D1461674

BBC

DOCTOR WHO

THE THIRTEENTH
DOCTOR'S GUIDE

PUFFIN

BBC CHILDREN'S BOOKS

UK | USA | Canada | Ireland | Australia
India | New Zealand | South Africa

BBC Children's Books are published by Puffin Books,
part of the Penguin Random House group of companies
whose addresses can be found at global.penguinrandomhouse.com.

www.penguin.co.uk
www.puffin.co.uk
www.ladybird.co.uk

A version of this book was first published in 2013 as
Doctor Who: The Essential Guide to Fifty Years of Doctor Who
and reissued in 2018 as *Doctor Who: The Handbook*
This updated edition published in 2020 as *Doctor Who: The Thirteenth Doctor's Guide*

001

Written by Justin Richards and Julian Richards
With thanks to Derek Handley
Copyright © BBC, 2013, 2018, 2020

Printed in China
A CIP catalogue record for this book is available from the British Library

ISBN: 978–1–405–94582–0

All correspondence to:
BBC Children's Books
Penguin Random House Children's
One Embassy Gardens, New Union Square
5 Nine Elms Lane, London SW8 5DA

CONTENTS

ADVENTURE
IN SPACE AND TIME

The first-ever episode of *Doctor Who* was broadcast by the BBC at 5.15pm on Saturday 23rd November 1963. A television legend was born.

Now, over fifty years later, we can look back and see an unrivalled success that the original producers of the programme and the people who watched it could never have imagined. The first mass television audience was for the 1953 coronation of Queen Elizabeth II – only ten years before. The idea that any TV series could last for so long was simply unthinkable.

But *Doctor Who* has always done the unthinkable, the impossible, things that no one else has even dreamed of. There is nothing else like it on television – there never has been and there never will be. Just like the Doctor, the series is unique.

No single book can ever give the full story of *Doctor Who* on television – never mind the thousands of other stories about the Doctor in comics, novels, short stories, audio adventures and even movies. But in this book we will cover the most important, the most essential, moments of the Doctor's enthralling journey through eternity.

It's a journey that will go on forever.

HOW IT ALL BEGAN

No one person created *Doctor Who*. The concept grew out of the work of many people, and a study by the BBC of science fiction and how it could work on television. At the same time, they were looking for a programme that would appeal to children as well as adults on a Saturday afternoon.

The most important people involved – out of many – were Sydney Newman, who was the BBC's new Head of Drama, Verity Lambert, who was appointed as the Producer of *Doctor Who*, writer Cecil E. Webber, who developed the early concepts and characters, and Anthony Coburn, who built on that work when he wrote the first episodes. Of course, the contribution of the initial cast, especially William Hartnell as the First Doctor, was also vital to the show's success.

Almost as soon as it had started, *Doctor Who* changed. In just the second story, the Doctor met the Daleks – and nothing would ever be the same again. Originally, *Doctor Who* was intended to alternate between science fiction and historical drama. But as soon as the Daleks appeared – created by writer Terry Nation and designed by Raymond P. Cusick from Nation's descriptions – history was destined to take second place to the monsters.

When William Hartnell left the lead role in 1966, it could all have ended. But the production team came up with the idea of 'regeneration' (though they didn't call it that at the time). The Doctor became a new man, played by a new actor. This was a narrative device that ensured the programme could run for all of time.

Sadly, though, it didn't. In 1989, BBC executives decided to give the Doctor a rest. It was a rest that lasted, apart from a brief return for the Eighth Doctor in 1996, up until 2005.

It is easier to attribute the success of the current series to one person. Writer Russell T Davies, a lifelong fan of *Doctor Who*, brought the series back bigger, bolder and better than ever. He reinvented the programme for the 21st century and established a style, format and quality that enabled his successor, Steven Moffat, to ensure that *Doctor Who* remained one of the most respected and successful television drama series in the world. It is a legacy that has now passed to new lead writer, Chris Chibnall.

THE FIRST DOCTOR

When he was younger, the Doctor was a much older man than he is now. The First Doctor was elderly and irritable, apt to lose his temper with his companions. He didn't suffer fools gladly. But he exhibited all the wisdom and desire for justice of later Doctors.

When he first appeared, travelling with his granddaughter, Susan, the Doctor was an enigma – his companions didn't even know where he came from. At first, he was wary of more company – and even blamed Ian and Barbara for sabotaging the TARDIS. But gradually he came to appreciate and value their company, especially after Susan's departure . . .

WHO IS THE FIRST DOCTOR?

William Hartnell was the first actor to play the Doctor. Born in 1908, Hartnell was a well-known screen actor. But his reputation was for playing 'tough guy' roles. He was an unlikely but inspired choice for the part of the mysterious Doctor.

Suffering from ill health, William Hartnell left the role in 1966. He returned for the tenth anniversary story *The Three Doctors* in 1972/3, but was too frail to work in the studio with the other Doctors. He died in April 1975.

ADVENTURES IN SPACE AND TIME

For the very first stories there was no overall title. *An Unearthly Child* is also sometimes called *100,000 BC*. *The Daleks* is sometimes called *The Dead Planet* or *The Mutants*. *The Edge of Destruction* is also known as *Inside the Spaceship*.

AN UNEARTHLY CHILD

Two teachers at Coal Hill School – Ian Chesterton and Barbara Wright – are concerned about one of their pupils. Susan Foreman seems incredibly clever, but her knowledge of some basic facts is strangely lacking.

Ian and Barbara follow Susan home, and find that she apparently lives with her grandfather in a junkyard at the end of Totter's Lane. Barbara and Ian force their way inside a police telephone box where they believe the old man who calls himself the Doctor is keeping Susan. The police box is the TARDIS, and the Doctor insists he can't let the teachers leave as they will bring future knowledge to the present day.

The TARDIS takes them all back in time to Earth's distant past. The travellers are captured by a primitive tribe that has lost the secret of fire. They have to work together to escape . . .

THE DALEKS

The TARDIS lands on the planet Skaro – in the middle of a petrified jungle. The planet has been devastated by nuclear war. The Doctor and his friends discover a vast metal city, and inside they meet the Daleks for the very first time.

Survivors of the war, the Daleks live inside protective survival machines. Their machines pick up static power from the metal floors so they cannot leave the city. The Daleks send Susan to take a message to the Thals – their foes, now mutated into blonde humanoids. Susan tells the Thals the Daleks are offering them food and supplies. But it is a trap – the Daleks' only interest in the Thals is their total extermination.

The Doctor and his friends warn the Thals of the danger, and manage to destroy the city's power source – disabling the Daleks.

THE TIME MEDDLER

The TARDIS lands on a beach in 1066, close to where King Harold will defeat Viking invaders at the Battle of Stamford Bridge. But the Doctor, Vicki and Steven are not the only time travellers there.

The Doctor discovers that the single monk at the local monastery has a TARDIS. He is a time meddler from Gallifrey, who thinks Harold would make a better king than William the Conqueror and plans to destroy the Viking fleet before it lands. That way, Harold won't exhaust his troops marching north to fight them and will win the Battle of Hastings.

The Doctor prevents the monk from interfering, and sabotages his TARDIS.

The earliest *Doctor Who* stories had different titles for each episode.

Mission to the Unknown was a one-episode prequel to *The Daleks' Master Plan* – a complete adventure without the Doctor or any of his companions. And the Daleks win!

THE DALEKS' MASTER PLAN

On the planet Kembel, the Daleks are forming an alliance with other alien races. Also at the conference is Mavic Chen, the traitorous Guardian of the Solar System. He has provided the Taranium Core of the Daleks' most deadly weapon: the Time Destructor.

The Doctor steals the vital core and escapes. Katarina gives her life to help the Doctor get away, but the Daleks chase the Doctor, Steven and agent Sara Kingdom through time and space. After a battle amongst the pyramids of ancient Egypt, the Doctor is forced to hand over the vital core.

Back on Kembel, the Doctor turns the Daleks' Time Destructor against them – tragically killing Sara who is caught in the weapon's destructive field.

Although Susan was a 15-year-old schoolgirl, Carole Ann Ford was in her twenties when she played the role.

SUSAN FOREMAN
Helped the Doctor
From: Before *An Unearthly Child*
Until: *The Dalek Invasion of Earth*
Played by: Carole Ann Ford

Susan was the Doctor's granddaughter. She took her surname from the name on the gates of the junkyard where the TARDIS was 'parked' – I M Foreman. Though she looked like a teenager and attended Coal Hill School, Susan displayed the knowledge and insight of a different age…

Jacqueline Hill later returned to *Doctor Who* playing a different character – Lexa in *Meglos*.

BARBARA WRIGHT
Helped the Doctor
From: *An Unearthly Child*
Until: *The Chase*
Played by: Jacqueline Hill

History teacher at Coal Hill School, Barbara was intrigued by the gaps and the depths of Susan's knowledge, and persuaded her colleague Ian Chesterton to investigate with her. She became an unwilling adventurer, but her common sense and determination were invaluable to the Doctor.

IAN CHESTERTON
Helped the Doctor
From: *An Unearthly Child*
Until: *The Chase*
Played by: William Russell

Science teacher at Coal Hill School, Ian went with his friend and colleague Barbara to the junkyard where the enigmatic Susan claimed to live. At first he was unable to accept that the TARDIS is a time-and-space machine, but once he came to terms with that he revelled in his adventures with the Doctor – though like Barbara he longed to get home again.

VICKI
Helped the Doctor
From: *The Rescue*
Until: *The Myth Makers*
Played by: Maureen O'Brien

An orphan girl from a future spaceship crash, adopted by the Doctor.

STEVEN TAYLOR

Helped the Doctor
From: *The Chase*
Until: *The Savages*
Played by: Peter Purves

A space pilot from the far future, rescued by the Doctor from battling Daleks and Mechonoids.

Peter Purves, who played Steven Taylor, went on to become one of the best-remembered presenters of *Blue Peter*.

KATARINA

Helped the Doctor
From: *The Myth Makers*
Until: *The Daleks' Master Plan*
Played by: Adrienne Hill

Handmaiden to High Priestess Cassandra in ancient Troy, Katarina sacrificed herself to allow the Doctor and Steven to escape from the Daleks in a stolen spaceship.

DODO CHAPLET

Helped the Doctor
From: *The Massacre*
Until: *The War Machines*
Played by: Jackie Lane

A London teenager who stumbled into the TARDIS.

POLLY

Helped the Doctor
From: *The War Machines*
Until: *The Faceless Ones*
Played by: Anneke Wills

Secretary to Professor Brett, she tried to return Dodo's TARDIS key to the Doctor.

SARA KINGDOM

Helped the Doctor
In: *The Daleks' Master Plan*
Played by: Jean Marsh

A space security agent, Sara was tricked into killing her own brother by the treacherous Mavic Chen, who was working for the Daleks. Sara was killed by the Daleks' Time Destructor.

BEN JACKSON

Helped the Doctor
From: *The War Machines*
Until: *The Faceless Ones*
Played by: Michael Craze

A merchant seaman and friend of Polly.

THE FIRST DOCTOR'S FOES

Top BBC executives thought the Daleks were 'bug-eyed monsters' that would take *Doctor Who* in the wrong direction and wanted their first story dropped – but luckily there wasn't time to write a new story to replace it.

THE DALEKS

The Doctor first encountered the Daleks on the planet Skaro. Mutated by centuries of warfare against the now-peaceful Thals, the creatures were housed inside robotic, armoured travel machines which could not move outside their metal city. Later, the Doctor defeated the Daleks when they invaded Earth in the 22nd century. In retaliation, the Daleks sent an assassination squad to pursue the TARDIS through time and space. The First Doctor's final encounter with the Daleks was when he used their Time Destructor to defeat them on the planet Kembel.

THE SENSORITES

Telepathic humanoids from the Sense Sphere.

THE VOORD

Led by Yartek, the Voord tried to take control of the Conscience Machine that controlled law and order on the planet Marinus. But one of the keys they used turned out to be a fake, and the machine was destroyed.

THE SLYTHER

Slimy, revolting and ferocious 'pet' of the Black Dalek used to guard the Bedfordshire mines.

THE MOROKS
The once-powerful race that built the Space Museum on the planet Xeros.

KOQUILLION
The apparent protector of a fearful Vicki on planet Dido, this tusked creature was not what he seemed.

ELAKIR
Saracen warlord who kidnapped Barbara for his harem.

When *Doctor Who* first started, stories alternated between science fiction and historical adventures.

The Mechonoids only appeared in one television story, *The Chase*, but became recurring comic-strip enemies of the Daleks.

THE ZARBI
The once-peaceful Zarbi were controlled by an alien intelligence, the Animus, which turned them against their fellow inhabitants of Vortis, the Menoptra. The Zarbi were like giant beetles or ants, while the Menoptra were humanoid butterflies. The Zarbi used scuttling grubs as weapons that could spit burning venom.

THE MECHONOIDS
Spherical robots sent out to prepare planets for human colonisation. They were armed with flame-throwers.

THE TENTH PLANET

The TARDIS arrives at the coldest place on Earth – close to the International Space Command Snowcap Base in Antarctica. The base is monitoring a manned space flight when a new planet appears – a planet that looks very like Earth.

It is Earth's lost twin planet Mondas, home of the Cybermen. The Cybermen are humans who have gradually replaced their bodies with artificial limbs and organs made of metal and plastic. They have also altered their brains so that they are now logical beings, with no emotions at all.

Mondas is absorbing energy – draining it away from Earth. A group of Cybermen take over Snowcap Base. They want to use a powerful Z Bomb to destroy Earth before Mondas absorbs too much energy.

Ben discovers the Cybermen are vulnerable to radiation, and the crew of the base defeat the Cybermen there. With the bomb disarmed, Mondas explodes, and the Cybermen remaining on Earth collapse and die.

The Doctor also collapses – his elderly body exhausted and worn out. The Doctor manages to get back to the TARDIS. But, to the astonishment of his companions Ben and Polly, he changes into a brand-new form . . .

REGENERATION

The First Doctor mellowed over the years after meeting Ian and Barbara. By the time he regenerated, he was less irascible and more inclined to see the good in others and help them. This may have been partly due to the emotional wrench of losing his granddaughter Susan, who stayed behind to make a new life on the ruined Earth of the 22nd century after the Doctor helped defeat the invading Daleks.

But as he grew perhaps more 'human' the Doctor also grew older. His body was wearing out and he got increasingly tired. By the time he faced the threat of invading Cybermen along with his new friends Ben and Polly, the Doctor was close to exhaustion.

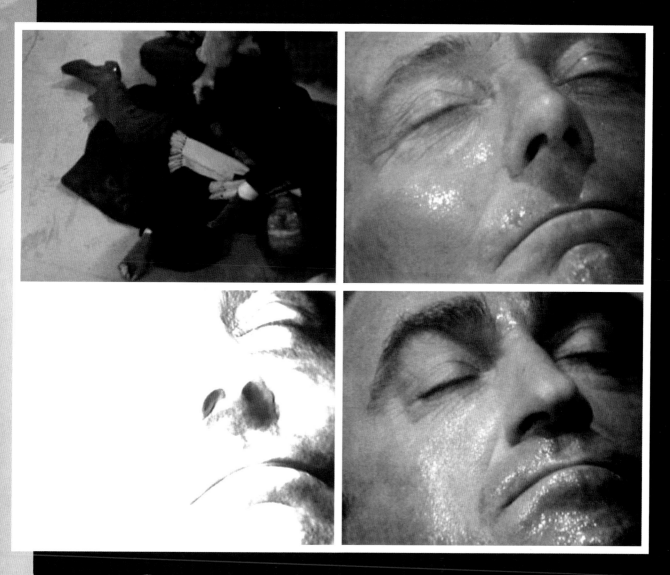

THE SECOND DOCTOR

The Second Doctor was a distinct contrast to the First. He was much younger, and seemed like a different person in almost every way. The First Doctor's short temper was replaced with a forgiving good humour. Wisdom seemed to have given way to an amateurish combination of guesswork and luck.

But this was a bluff, an act, on the part of the Doctor. Beneath the surface was the same passion for justice and fairness. His humour could give way to a deep anger at his enemies, and the bluster and apparent reliance on luck masked the same depth of knowledge and ability as the Doctor has always displayed. Everything about the Second Doctor invited his enemies to underestimate him – and they did so at their peril.

WHO IS THE SECOND DOCTOR?

The actor given the daunting task of taking over from William Hartnell in the role of the Doctor was Patrick Troughton. Born in 1920, Troughton was an established and talented character actor, and initially had doubts about whether he could follow in Hartnell's footsteps.

After discussing several ideas about how to play the role, Patrick Troughton eventually decided to make the Doctor an intergalactic wanderer – a 'cosmic hobo'. He created an entirely new persona that was still true to the core of the character. After three years of full-time Doctoring, Troughton left the role, although he returned for *The Three Doctors* (1972/3), *The Five Doctors* (1983) and *The Two Doctors* (1985). He died in 1987.

THE TOMB OF THE CYBERMEN

On Telos, Professor Parry's archaeological expedition is searching for the ancient lost remains of the legendary Cybermen. But the Cybermen are not extinct, as was thought. They are frozen in huge tombs beneath the city. Two of the expedition, Kaftan and Klieg, plan to revive the Cybermen and work with them to conquer humanity.

The Doctor traps the Cybermen, but they despatch deadly Cybermats and convert Toberman, Kaftan's servant, so that he is part-Cyberman. The Doctor seals the Cybermen back into their tombs, and the Cyber Controller is destroyed.

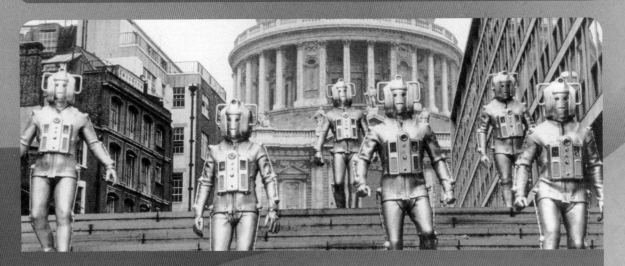

THE INVASION

The Doctor, Jamie and Zoe again meet Lethbridge-Stewart – now a brigadier, in charge of the newly formed UNIT (United Nations Intelligence Taskforce) organisation. UNIT is investigating International Electromatics – the world's biggest electronics manufacturer – and its enigmatic managing director, Tobias Vaughn.

Vaughn is in league with the Cybermen, who are planning an invasion. A hypnotic signal is transmitted through the micromonolithic circuits present in all IE's products. Earth is paralysed, and the Cybermen emerge from hiding in the London sewers to invade.

The Doctor persuades Vaughn to help defeat the Cybermen. Zoe helps the RAF destroy the Cyber-fleet, and UNIT redirects a Russian missile to destroy the main Cyber ship.

Many of the First and Second Doctor's episodes are missing from the BBC Archives, including most of *The Evil of the Daleks* and *The Abominable Snowmen*.

THE ICE WARRIORS

The Doctor, Jamie and Victoria arrive in the snowy wastes of a new ice age, just as an ancient warrior is found encased in ice and excavated from the glacier. Revived, Varga the 'Ice Warrior' kidnaps Victoria and awakens the crew of his spaceship, which crashed on the glacier centuries ago. Varga realises that his own world – Mars – must be long dead, and decides to make Earth their new planet.

THE WEB OF FEAR

The TARDIS lands in the London Underground. But the city has been evacuated after a strange mist appeared above ground, coalescing into 'web' in the tunnels beneath the city. The Great Intelligence is back (after *The Abominable Snowmen*), with its robot Yeti servants. The Doctor and his friends work with the military, led by Colonel Lethbridge-Stewart, to defeat the Great Intelligence.

The Evil of the Daleks was intended to be the last-ever Dalek story – so that their creator Terry Nation could set up a Dalek TV series. But funding problems meant it was never made.

THE EVIL OF THE DALEKS

The Daleks plan to synthesise the 'Human Factor' so they can understand why humans have defeated them, and force the Doctor to record Jamie's emotions and reactions when he rescues Victoria Waterfield. From this they can distil the Human Factor.

The Dalek Emperor reveals that the Doctor has actually distilled the 'Dalek Factor' – the impulse to exterminate – which they will now spread through Earth history. But the Doctor 'infects' some Daleks with the Human Factor and they begin to question the orders of their Black Dalek leaders.

When she was cast as Polly, actress Anneke Wills was married to actor Michael Gough – who played the First Doctor's adversary the Celestial Toymaker.

POLLY

Helped the Doctor
From: *The War Machines*
Until: *The Faceless Ones*
Played by: *Anneke Wills*

Having travelled with both the First and Second Doctors, Polly finally left the TARDIS on the same day she first entered it.

Jamie and Zoe were sent back to their own times by the Time Lords – with no memory of their adventures with the Doctor after their first encounter.

BEN JACKSON

Helped the Doctor
From: *The War Machines*
Until: *The Faceless Ones*
Played by: *Michael Craze*

A companion to the First and Second Doctors, Ben left the TARDIS with Polly at Gatwick Airport.

JAMIE McCRIMMON

Helped the Doctor
From: *The Highlanders*
Until: *The War Games*
Played by: *Frazer Hines*

James Robert McCrimmon first met the Doctor in 1746 after the Battle of Culloden, which ended the Jacobite Rebellion. Though he didn't understand the sophisticated technology of the TARDIS, he had a great deal of common sense and a practical outlook. Above all, Jamie was brave and steadfast – never one to step back from a fight. He became one of the Doctor's best friends, and his longest-serving companion. He was eventually sent back to his own time by the Time Lords.

VICTORIA WATERFIELD

Helped the Doctor
From: *The Evil of the Daleks*
Until: *Fury from the Deep*
Played by: Deborah Watling

When Victoria's father was killed by the Daleks, the Doctor promised he would look after her. From 1866, Victoria, like Jamie, did not understand everything she experienced on her travels with the Doctor, and was a somewhat reluctant adventurer. Kind and intelligent, she was often the voice of calm and reason in the TARDIS. She left when she had the offer of a quiet, 'normal' life in the 1960s.

Jack Watling, who played Travers in *The Abominable Snowmen* and *The Web of Fear*, is the father of Deborah Watling, who played Victoria.

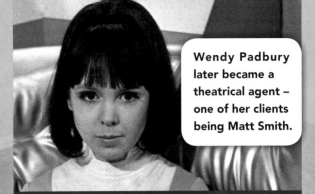

Wendy Padbury later became a theatrical agent – one of her clients being Matt Smith.

ZOE HERIOT

Helped the Doctor
From: *The Wheel in Space*
Until: *The War Games*
Played by: Wendy Padbury

Zoe was a young astrophysicist and astrometricist on Station Three – nicknamed the Wheel in Space. After helping the Doctor and Jamie defeat an attack by the Cybermen, she hid on board the TARDIS. The Doctor showed her how he and Jamie battled against the Daleks (in *The Evil of the Daleks*) but she was still keen to travel with them. She was eventually sent back to her own time by the Time Lords.

COLONEL/BRIGADIER ALISTAIR GORDON LETHBRIDGE-STEWART

Helped the Doctor
In: *The Web of Fear*
The Invasion
Played by: Nicholas Courtney

A career soldier, Lethbridge-Stewart was given the task of combating the Great Intelligence when its Yeti attacked London. The experience led to his appointment as the head of the British contingent of UNIT and promotion to brigadier.

THE SECOND DOCTOR'S FOES

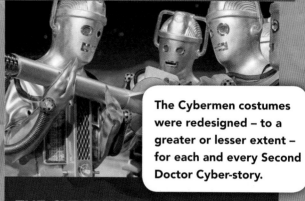

The Cybermen costumes were redesigned – to a greater or lesser extent – for each and every Second Doctor Cyber-story.

THE DALEKS

Immediately after his regeneration, the Second Doctor came up against the Daleks. But these were Daleks that seemed subservient to the human colonists on planet Vulcan – and who recognised the new Doctor. Only the Doctor seemed to realise that the Daleks were watching, waiting, growing stronger – until they were powerful enough to 'exterminate all humans'. Later, the Daleks kidnapped the Doctor and forced him to create the Human Factor. On the Dalek home planet Skaro, he confronted the Dalek Emperor for the first time.

THE CYBERMEN

More than any other foe, the Second Doctor found himself pitted against the Cybermen. He managed to foil their attempt to take over the Moonbase and their plan to devastate Earth by controlling the planet's weather. The Doctor also witnessed the opening of the tombs of the Cybermen. Here he encountered Cybermats for the first time – small, rodent-like cybernetic creatures used by the Cybermen. They also used Cybermats to infiltrate the Wheel in Space. Finally, the Doctor and the newly formed UNIT managed to defeat a Cyber-invasion of Earth.

THE MACRA

Hiding in the darkness, the Macra were huge creatures resembling crabs that secretly controlled a human colony, manipulating the people into mining the gas the creatures needed to survive.

FISH PEOPLE

In the sunken kingdom of Atlantis, shipwrecked sailors and others who strayed into this underwater realm were converted into Fish People – sent out to gather food for the inhabitants.

All the Second Doctor's stories start with 'The' except one – *Fury from the Deep.*

THE CHAMELEONS

A race of aliens that lost their identities in an accident on their homeworld. The Chameleons stole identities from people they kidnapped on planes leaving Gatwick Airport and took to their space station.

THE DALEK EMPEROR

On Skaro, the Doctor confronted the Emperor Dalek – a vast monolithic structure built into the Dalek City. The Dalek Emperor tried to force the Doctor to take the Dalek Factor back to Earth and spread it through all human history, but instead the Doctor managed to 'humanise' a faction of Daleks and civil war broke out on Skaro. The Emperor was destroyed in the conflict – or so the Doctor believed . . .

THE GREAT INTELLIGENCE & YETI

A formless, ethereal being, the Great Intelligence sought to find form and identity on Earth. From its first (so far as the Doctor knew) attempts to invade in Tibet, the Great Intelligence created robot Yeti, each controlled by a silver sphere. After the Intelligence was defeated, explorer Travers brought back several control spheres and a Yeti to London – giving the Intelligence all it needed to set a trap for the Doctor and invade again . . .

When he was put on trial by the Time Lords, the Doctor showed them some of the evils he had fought – Daleks, Cybermen, Yeti and Quarks.

SALAMANDER

A powerful politician and scientist, Salamander was not the benevolent dictator he seemed to be. But his close resemblance meant the Doctor could impersonate him to discover his true plans.

DOMINATORS & QUARKS

The Dominators were a race of ruthless expansionists, conquering other planets. Their 'soldiers' were the deadly robot Quarks. The Doctor managed to defeat their attack on the peaceful planet Dulkis – which they intended to blow up to provide a fuel source for their invasion fleet.

ICE WARRIORS

Originally natives of the planet Mars, the so-called Ice Warriors were looking for a new home – and set their sights on Earth. The first Ice Warriors that the Doctor encountered were survivors of a spaceship crash, thawed out in a future ice age. An Ice Warrior fleet also tried to invade Earth in the late 21st century, having taken over a moonbase and sent deadly poisonous Martian seed pods to Earth to change the atmosphere.

The small robot Quarks were 'operated' by schoolchildren.

MIND ROBBER

In one of his strangest adventures, the Doctor found himself transported to a world of fictional characters controlled by a vast computer. He encountered storybook characters including Gulliver, Rapunzel, Medusa, a unicorn, the minotaur . . . and an army of life-sized clockwork robots.

THE WAR LORD

Helped by a rogue Time Lord – the War Chief – a group of aliens led by the War Lord kidnapped human soldiers from throughout history to form their own army.

The War Lord's people had limited-use time machines, designed by the War Chief and referred to (though only once) as SIDRATs.

KROTONS

A crystalline life-form, the Krotons sapped the life energy of the Gonds to reconstitute themselves.

THE WAR GAMES

The TARDIS arrives in the middle of the First World War. Or so it seems. The Doctor is accused of being a German spy and sentenced to be shot by firing squad. But he is saved by a redcoat soldier from the 18th century! Before long, the Doctor, Jamie and Zoe are being charged at by Roman soldiers . . .

They are not on Earth at all, but in the middle of 'war games' – re-enactments of Earth wars organised by the alien War Lord. With the help of a rogue Time Lord, the aliens are using the war games to select the best soldiers. They will form these into a huge brainwashed army.

The Doctor defeats the aliens, but the only way he can get the thousands of stranded humans home is by calling in his own people – the Time Lords. Although he tries to escape, the Doctor is caught and put on trial for interfering in other planets and times. The Time Lords wipe Jamie's and Zoe's memory of all but their first adventure with the Doctor and send them home. The Doctor is exiled to Earth in the 20th century, with a new appearance and without the expertise he needs to escape in the TARDIS . . .

REGENERATION

The Second Doctor's character remained largely unchanged over the years, although he did gradually calm down a little. At first, he seemed to be vague and dithering, but by the time he faced the War Lord and his own people, his companions had come to realise how clever and ingenious the Doctor really was beneath this façade. However, in his own people – the Time Lords – the Doctor finally met his match. Once they knew where he was, they captured the TARDIS and put the Doctor on trial for the terrible crime of interfering in the affairs of other races . . .

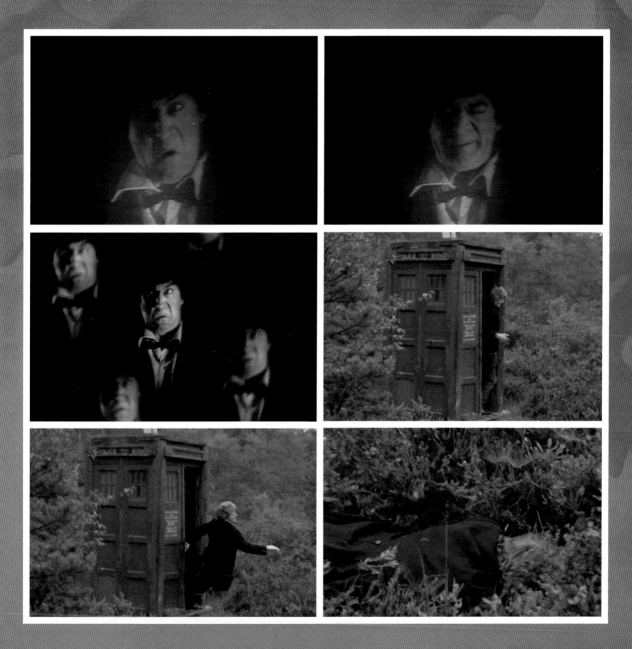

THE THIRD
DOCTOR

In contrast to his predecessor, the Third Doctor was a tall, suave, sophisticated man of action. More of an 'establishment' figure than any other incarnation, the Third Doctor spent his time – at first unwillingly – as Scientific Adviser to UNIT. He was a scientist, a raconteur, a bon vivant. Like the First Doctor he never suffered fools gladly – especially bureaucrats and civil servants.

The Third Doctor was also perhaps the most physical, dispatching opponents with his own brand of Venusian Aikido. Again unlike his predecessors, he did not shun technology but revelled in it – intrigued by gadgets and losing no opportunity to build some scientific device to do anything from open a door to detect delta particles or a rogue TARDIS.

WHO IS THE THIRD DOCTOR?

When he was cast as the Doctor, Jon Pertwee was best known for his acting work on radio and his ability to create a variety of different characters with his vocal talents. Born in 1919, he had also appeared in films – including *Carry on Screaming* where he played the scientist Dr Fettle. He was almost exclusively a comic actor, but approached the character of the Doctor as a serious dramatic role.

Jon Pertwee left *Doctor Who* after five years, returning for the 1983 anniversary story *The Five Doctors*. He died in 1996, and is best remembered for the roles of scarecrow Worzel Gummidge and of course the Third Doctor.

THE SEA DEVILS

The Doctor and Jo visit the Master who is being held in a high-security prison on an island. While there, they discover that ships have been mysteriously sinking in the local waters.

Right in the middle of this area is an abandoned sea fort, which is being converted into a sonar test station. When they go to the fort, the Doctor and Jo are attacked by a 'Sea Devil' – a marine 'cousin' of the Silurians.

The Master has contacted the Sea Devils. They rescue him from prison, and capture the Doctor. The Doctor offers to negotiate a peace with the human race, but his efforts are disrupted by an attack by the Royal Navy.

As the Master incites the Sea Devils to war, and the Navy battles against their attacks, the Doctor has no choice but to destroy the Sea Devil colony.

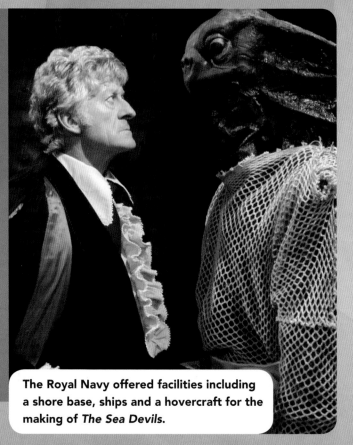

The Royal Navy offered facilities including a shore base, ships and a hovercraft for the making of *The Sea Devils*.

SPEARHEAD FROM SPACE

Exiled to Earth in the 20th century by the Time Lords, the Doctor's arrival coincides with a strange meteor shower which is being investigated by UNIT. The recovering Doctor soon meets his old friend Brigadier Lethbridge-Stewart.

They discover that the Nestenes are planning to invade – replacing politicians and military figures with Auton duplicates. Killer Autons – deadly plastic mannequins – have been distributed to shops across the country. As the Autons attack, the Doctor and UNIT infiltrate the plastics factory where the Nestenes are based. Their leader, Channing, is creating a monstrous plastic creature that will house the bulk of the Nestene Consciousness. As UNIT battles the Autons, the Doctor and his assistant Liz Shaw manage to destroy the creature, and the Nestenes withdraw their consciousness.

Spearhead from Space was the first *Doctor Who* story broadcast in colour – and, because of a BBC strike, the only story of the 'classic' series to be shot entirely on film, rather than mainly on videotape.

The writer of *The Daemons* – Guy Leopold – is actually a pseudonym for series producer Barry Letts and writer Robert Sloman.

THE DAEMONS

The Doctor and Jo visit the village of Devil's End where an archaeologist is excavating an ancient burial mound called The Devil's Hump. The Doctor is knocked unconscious by a blast of cold air as the mound is opened.

When he recovers, the village is enclosed in a heat barrier. The Doctor enlists the help of Miss Hawthorne, a local white witch, to battle against an animated church gargoyle, hostile villagers and sinister Morris dancers . . . They also discover that the local vicar is actually the Master in disguise.

He plans to summon Azal, the last Daemon – the creature that was dormant inside the mound. Azal is ready to assess how his race's 'experiment' to influence human evolution has gone. If it is deemed a failure, he will destroy the world. If not, he will pass on his great power – which is what the Master is after.

Azal prepares to kill the Doctor, but Jo's offer to take his place so confuses the Daemon that he is destroyed. The Master is captured by UNIT and taken away to stand trial . . .

THE THREE DOCTORS

The power of the Time Lords is being drained away into a mysterious black hole. Their only hope is the exiled Doctor – all three of him!

On Earth, UNIT finds itself besieged by strange gelatinous creatures that also seem to be hunting for the Doctor. The Time Lords bring the first three incarnations of the Doctor together, although the First Doctor is only able to communicate through the TARDIS scanner.

Together, the Doctors travel through the black hole, to a world of anti-matter. Here they discover that Omega – the Time Lords' stellar engineer who provided the power source that gave them time travel – has survived. Now he wants to escape from the black hole and take revenge on the Time Lords who he believes abandoned and betrayed him.

With Omega defeated and his world destroyed, the Doctors return to their own times . . .

When infiltrating the Global Chemicals organisation in *The Green Death*, the Doctor disguises himself first as an elderly milkman, then as a cleaning-woman.

THE GREEN DEATH

UNIT investigates a mysterious death at a disused coal-mine, close to the headquarters of Global Chemicals. Working with a local group of ecologists, the Doctor discovers that Global Chemicals has been dumping toxic waste down the mine. The waste kills anyone who touches it, and has caused maggots to mutate and grow in size.

UNIT tries to contain a plague of maggots that burrows up from the mine. Meanwhile, the Doctor gets inside Global Chemicals. He finds the real head of the organisation is a megalomaniac computer called BOSS that has the ability to control people's minds and is planning world domination.

The Doctor manages to destroy BOSS, but now he has to stop the maggots before they metamorphose into giant flies that spit poisonous chemical waste.

THE TIME WARRIOR

When several of the country's leading scientists disappear, UNIT gathers together the others – including the Doctor. One of the 'scientists' turns out to be journalist Sarah Jane Smith, who hides inside the TARDIS when the Doctor follows the kidnapper – to medieval times.

The culprit is Linx, a Sontaran who has crash-landed. Using his ship's osmic projector, he has brought back scientists from the 20th century to repair his ship. As a reward to Irongron, the robber baron who is sheltering him, Linx provides rifles and even a robot knight.

Hoping to stop this dangerous interference with the course of history, the Doctor tries to reason with Linx, but without success. Linx is killed by an archer as he tries to take off in his repaired ship. The resulting explosion destroys Irongron's castle, together with all the modern technology Linx provided.

BRIGADIER ALISTAIR GORDON LETHBRIDGE-STEWART

Helped the Doctor
From: *Spearhead from Space*
Until: *Terror of the Zygons* (intermittently)
Played by: *Nicholas Courtney*

Head of the UK contingent of UNIT, the Brigadier recruited the Doctor to help Liz Shaw as the organisation's Scientific Adviser. He was initially wary of the new Doctor, not sure if it could really be the same person. But the Doctor's undeniable scientific brilliance and eccentricity soon persuaded him. The Brigadier enjoyed a friendship with the Doctor that could be frosty at times as their outlooks and approaches were very different – a point brought home when the Brigadier destroyed the Silurians' base while the Doctor favoured peace negotiations.

LIZ SHAW

Helped the Doctor
From: *Spearhead from Space*
Until: *Inferno*
Played by: *Caroline John*

UNIT's first Scientific Adviser, Doctor Elizabeth Shaw was recruited from Cambridge University by the Brigadier. Initially sceptical about 'little blue men with three heads', she was forced to revise her opinions when she met the Doctor and battled the Autons.

Benton first appeared in the Second Doctor story *The Invasion* – as a UNIT corporal. Actor John Levene was also in *The Web of Fear* – but as a Yeti!

SERGEANT BENTON

Helped the Doctor
From: *The Invasion*
Until: *The Android Invasion* (intermittently)
Played by: *John Levene*

One of the longest-serving and most loyal members of UNIT, Benton became a firm friend of the Doctor.

Actress Katy Manning is extremely short-sighted, but played the role of Jo Grant without her glasses.

JO GRANT

Helped the Doctor
From: *Terror of the Autons*
Until: *The Green Death*
Played by: *Katy Manning*

Hardly the most typical of UNIT operatives, Josephine Grant got a job with the organisation through what the Brigadier described as 'friends in high places' – in fact, her uncle. But after getting off on the wrong foot when Jo accidentally ruined an experiment of the Doctor's, the two soon became great friends. Jo finally left the Doctor – and UNIT – to marry Professor Cliff Jones.

CAPTAIN YATES

Helped the Doctor
From: *Terror of the Autons*
Until: *Planet of the Spiders* (intermittently)
Played by: *Richard Franklin*

The Brigadier's second in command for much of the time at UNIT, Mike Yates was forced to resign after betraying the organisation. He returned, as  a civilian, to help battle against the giant spiders of Metebelis Three.

SARAH JANE SMITH

Helped the Doctor
From: *The Time Warrior*
Until: *The Hand of Fear*
Played by: *Elisabeth Sladen*

Journalist Sarah Jane Smith took the place of her scientist aunt Lavinia to get into a secret UNIT location. If she was looking for a story, she certainly got one – though she could never publish it – as she was soon whisked back to medieval times to face a stranded Sontaran warrior. But Sarah soon proved her worth and became one of the Doctor's closest and dearest friends.

Actress April Walker was first cast as Sarah Jane Smith, but it was later decided she wasn't quite right for the role and Elisabeth Sladen got the part.

THE THIRD DOCTOR'S FOES

NESTENES & AUTONS

A formless collective intelligence, the Nestenes colonised other planets for a million years, then came to Earth. Animating plastic, they used shop-window dummies and killer Auton mannequins in their attempts to conquer the planet, as well as duplicates of important statesmen, politicians and military figures.

SILURIANS

Millions of years ago, the reptilian 'Silurians' were the dominant intelligent life-form on Earth. But faced with a vast natural disaster, they retreated into hibernation centres to sleep through the catastrophe. They had miscalculated, and the catastrophe never happened – so they slept on. When they woke, they believed that Earth was still their world, and that humans were merely apes with delusions of grandeur.

ALIEN AMBASSADORS

When British space mission Mars Probe 7 got into trouble, a recovery mission was sent to rescue the astronauts. But what returned to Earth was not human.

PRIMORDS AND PROFESSOR STAHLMAN

Project Inferno aimed to drill through the Earth's crust and tap into a reserve of energy-providing gas. But it also released poisonous fluid that turned everyone it touched into savage, primordial creatures.

THE MASTER

A renegade Time Lord, the Master was the antithesis of the Doctor in terms of his beliefs and goals. He revelled in destruction, and craved power. A formidable hypnotist and an expert at disguising himself, the Master joined forces with many of the Doctor's enemies in his attempts to gain power – including Axos, Sea Devils and even the Daleks . . .

AXOS & AXONS

Axos and the Axons were a single parasitic entity. The Axons appeared at first to be beautiful golden humanoids, offering the gift of axonite – a 'thinking molecule' that could solve problems like world starvation. But the Axons were really hideous tentacle creatures intent on draining all energy from Earth.

IMC

The Interplanetary Mining Corporation was an unscrupulous company that put profits above people. They tried to evict colonists from the planet Uxarieus – which was also home to an ancient Doomsday Weapon which the Master tried to find.

SEA DEVILS

An aquatic kind of Silurians, the Sea Devils – as they were nicknamed – allied themselves with the Master to try to regain 'their' planet.

AZAL THE DAEMON

The Daemons were an ancient and powerful race in the image of the traditional 'devil' that guided the development of humanity through the ages. The Master tried to persuade Azal, the last of the Daemons, to pass on his great power – but Azal decided to give it to the Doctor rather than the Master. The Doctor, of course, refused this 'gift'.

ARCTURUS AND AGGEDOR

On the planet Peladon, the Doctor and Jo met a group of alien delegates – including the hideous Arcturus, a grotesque head housed inside a life-support machine. They also encountered Aggedor, the fabled royal beast of Peladon, thought to be extinct.

DALEKS

The Third Doctor first encountered the Daleks when they established a time paradox that enabled them to invade Earth after a series of terrible wars. These were actually started by rebels returning through time to stop those same wars. Later, the Doctor found that the Daleks were behind a plot to set the empires of Earth and Draconia at war, and defeated their army on the planet Spiridon. Again in the future, the Doctor was forced into an alliance with Daleks on the planet Exxilon. But the Daleks re-armed themselves with machine-guns to take control.

MUTANTS

The inhabitants of the Earth colony planet Solos became hideous-looking mutant creatures as part of their natural life cycle. But the ruling humans – and other Solonians – believed it was a disease.

OGRONS

Ape-like servants of the Daleks, the Ogrons were used as security forces in a future Dalek-dominated Earth. The Master also used them to foment war between Earth and Draconia.

KRONOS

A Chronovore – a creature that eats time – living outside normal space-time, Kronos was worshipped in ancient Atlantis. The Master tried to enslave Kronos, but she escaped, destroying Atlantis.

> Drashig is an anagram of 'dish rag'.

DRASHIGS

Vicious omnivorous creatures from one of Grundle's satellites, the Drashigs will eat anything – but prefer meat.

BOSS & GIANT MAGGOTS

The Doctor and UNIT were called to South Wales to investigate a strange death connected with a disused coal-mine. Global Chemicals was pumping waste material from its new oil-refining process into the old mine – waste that was deadly to the touch and mutated maggots into monsters. The company turned out to be controlled by a giant computer – the first Bimorphic Organisational Systems Supervisor, or BOSS for short.

DINOSAURS

When the Doctor and Sarah returned from defeating the Sontaran Linx, they found London deserted – evacuated after dinosaurs started appearing throughout the city. The Doctor and UNIT managed to find the culprits – a misguided scientist and his allies who wanted to create a new 'golden age' for planet Earth by rolling back time millions of years.

OMEGA

The stellar engineer who provided the Time Lords with the power source they needed to achieve time travel, Omega was apparently destroyed in the supernova created by his work. But in fact, he survived within a black hole where he created a world controlled by the force of his will. When Omega took revenge on the Time Lords – who he thought had betrayed and abandoned him – the first three Doctors were brought together to defeat him.

SPIDERS

When the Doctor visited Metebelis Three, he found a blue crystal – but years later the giant spiders, mutated from a spider brought from Earth, wanted it back. It was the last perfect crystal of power, which an enormous spider called The Great One needed to complete a crystal lattice that would enhance her power infinitely.

SONTARANS

When Commander Linx, a Sontaran officer, crash-landed in medieval Britain, he used his damaged ship's osmic projector to kidnap scientists from the 20th century to help him make repairs. He also enlisted  the help of a local warlord. The Sontarans were a race of cloned warriors, bred for war against their enemy the Rutans.

DRACONIANS

Reptilian humanoids steeped in honour and tradition, the Draconians had an empire that bordered that of Earth. Misunderstanding and distrust led to a terrible war, but that was followed by many years of peaceful coexistence – until the Master and his Ogron servants tried to persuade each side that the other was attacking it. The Doctor was made a noble of Draconia 500 years earlier, after helping the Fifteenth Emperor cure a great space plague.

Jon Pertwee thought the Draconians were the most realistic of the alien life-forms he encountered.

ICE WARRIORS

Members of the Galactic Federation, the Ice Warriors seemed for once to be on the same side as the Doctor when they met on the planet Peladon. The Doctor was initially wary of Lord Izlyr and his deputy Ssorg. But together with the delegate from Alpha Centauri, the Doctor, Jo and the Ice Warriors managed to uncover a plot to stop Peladon  joining the Federation. Fifty years later, the Doctor encountered a faction of Ice Warriors that had returned to their old ways of death or glory. Led by Lord Azaxyr, they worked with a human traitor to betray the Federation to their enemies in Galaxy Five.

PLANET OF THE SPIDERS

A large blue crystal that the Doctor found on Metebelis Three and gave to Jo Grant as a wedding present (in *The Green Death*) is important to the giant spiders that live on the planet in the far future. They determine to get it back, and open a route to contemporary Earth. While Sarah and Mike Yates investigate the Meditation Centre where the spiders appear, the crystal is stolen by Lupton, who is in league with the spiders.

The Doctor and Sarah travel to Metebelis Three, where they discover the giant spiders need the crystal to deliver to The Great One. She is an enormous spider, living inside a huge crystal cave under the mountains.

The Doctor confronts The Great One, who is destroyed by the power of the crystal. But the Doctor's body is also destroyed by the crystal radiation. The TARDIS takes him back to Earth, where he regenerates under the ministrations of another Time Lord – his old mentor . . .

REGENERATION

The Third Doctor's era marked a distinct shift from the previous years of *Doctor Who*. For the first time, the programme was broadcast in colour, and the Doctor was – largely – confined to present-day Earth. But beneath these obvious changes, the Doctor remained the same. His friends and his place within rather than outside society had altered, but his motives and ambitions were unchanged. When he finally got back the use of his TARDIS and his exile was over, he couldn't wait to get out into the universe and continue his travels . . .

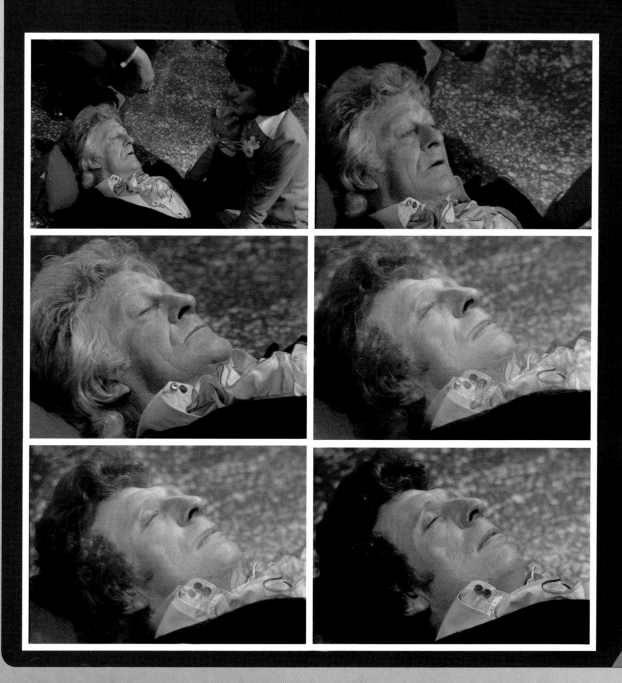

THE FOURTH
DOCTOR

The Fourth Doctor was perhaps the most 'alien' of all his incarnations. Sometimes aloof, always surprising, he constantly wrong-footed his enemies – and often his friends as well. He cut a distinctive figure with his wide-brimmed hat and long scarf, but his appearance was deceptive. He might have seemed like a Bohemian eccentric, but his mind was as sharp as ever. This was a Doctor whose breadth and depth of knowledge was unrivalled.

In amongst the mixture of wisdom and buffoonery there was a darkness. The Fourth Doctor was an often lonely wanderer in eternity. It was in the quiet moments, when the act dropped away, that we saw the real character of the Fourth Doctor. But for most of the time he seemed larger than life – a life into which he was determined to cram as much experience and incident as he possibly could.

WHO IS THE FOURTH DOCTOR?

Several actors were considered for the role of the Doctor when Jon Pertwee left the programme, but in Tom Baker the producers found an actor who delivered what many viewers and fans saw as the perfect Doctor.

Born in 1934, Baker had spent time in a monastery before turning to acting. He played various stage and film roles before finding himself out of work – and writing to Bill Slater, the BBC's Head of Serials, to ask for work. Slater recommended him to producer Barry Letts who went to see Baker as the villain in the film *The Golden Voyage of Sinbad*.

Almost as eccentric as the Doctor he portrayed, Tom Baker played the role for longer than any other actor. Since leaving the role, he has continued to work extensively on television.

The idea for *Genesis of the Daleks* came from departing producer Barry Letts, who suggested Dalek creator Terry Nation show where the Daleks originally came from.

GENESIS OF THE DALEKS

On the planet Skaro, the Thals and Kaleds have been at war for a thousand years. But now the brilliant Kaled scientist Davros has devised a travel machine for the mutated creatures his race will become. It is also a weapon that will win the war – the Dalek.

   The Doctor is unable to stop Davros's Daleks from all but destroying the Thals and then turning on their own creator. But the Doctor knows that out of the Daleks' evil will also come some good.

TERROR OF THE ZYGONS

A Zygon spaceship crashed into Loch Ness centuries ago, and the crew has remained hidden, depending on the milk of a huge armoured cyborg creature called a Skarasen – the Loch Ness Monster. Now the Zygons have discovered their home planet has been destroyed and plan to take over Earth for the Zygon refugees.

   The Zygons can imitate captured humans – and even imitate the Doctor's friend Harry. But with the help of the Brigadier and UNIT, the Doctor destroys the Zygon ship. With no Zygons to give it orders, the Skarasen returns to its 'home' – Loch Ness . . .

PYRAMIDS OF MARS

The TARDIS is drawn off course and arrives at Marcus Scarman's house in 1911. Scarman is an Egyptologist who has stumbled upon the tomb of the Osiran Sutekh, who kills him and uses his animated dead body to carry out his will.

A war criminal, Sutekh was imprisoned by his fellow Osirans beneath a pyramid in a forcefield controlled from Mars. The event became the basis for the ancient Egyptian gods and legends. Using service robots that look like Egyptian mummies, Sutekh plans to build a missile to destroy the power source that holds him prisoner. The Doctor and Sarah destroy the missile, but Sutekh escapes down a space-time corridor. The Doctor uses TARDIS technology to move the end of the corridor into the far future so that Sutekh ages to death before he can escape.

The Deadly Assassin was the first story in which the Doctor travels without a companion.

THE DEADLY ASSASSIN

The Doctor returns to Gallifrey for the President's Resignation. But when the President is assassinated, the Doctor is arrested for the crime. Behind the plot is the Master. He has used up all his regenerations and is close to death – an emaciated, wasted figure. He plans to use the power of the Eye of Harmony to restore his body to health. Framing the Doctor is a bonus.

The Doctor tracks down the Master's accomplice – Chancellor Goth. Inside the Matrix, the Time Lords' repository of all knowledge, Goth and the Doctor do battle in a nightmare world created from Goth's imagination. The Doctor wins, and is able to stop the Master before all of Gallifrey is sucked into a black hole. But the Master escapes.

THE TALONS OF WENG-CHIANG

On their way to a Victorian theatre, the Doctor and Leela encounter a group of Chinese ruffians from the Tong of the Black Scorpion, dedicated to the service of the great god Weng-Chiang.

The Tong is led by stage magician Li H'Sen Chang, who is performing at the Palace Theatre with his ventriloquist's dummy Mr Sin. But Sin is actually a homicidal robot from the far future with the brain of a pig. Both Sin and Chang work for Magnus Greel – a 51st-century war criminal who has escaped to 19th-century London and is searching for his lost time cabinet.

With the help of pathologist Professor Litefoot and theatre owner Henry Gordon Jago, the Doctor and Leela track Greel to the House of the Dragon, and manage to defeat both Greel and Mr Sin.

THE INVASION OF TIME

The Doctor returns to Gallifrey, after being accidentally elected President (in *The Deadly Assassin*). But he has Leela banished into the wastelands of Outer Gallifrey, and helps the Vardans to invade his home planet. The Vardans can travel along any waveform – even thought. The Doctor has banished Leela to keep her safe, and had the President's office lined with lead to shield his thoughts. Now he has forced the invaders to commit themselves, he can defeat them.

Just as victory seems certain, the Sontarans arrive. They were using the Vardans to gain access to Gallifrey, and hunt the Doctor through the rooms and corridors of the TARDIS. But the Doctor defeats them using a powerful Demat Gun.

Shada is the 'lost story' of *Doctor Who*. A six-part adventure written by Douglas Adams, it was to follow *The Horns of Nimon*. But industrial action at the BBC meant the story was never completed. What was actually shot is available on DVD, and the story can be experienced as a novel by Gareth Roberts.

THE KEY TO TIME

The White Guardian sends the Doctor and K-9 with the Time Lady Romana to find the six segments of the powerful Key to Time. The segments are disguised, and agents of the Black Guardian are also searching for them. Their quest takes the Doctor and his friends to a variety of dangerous times and places in an epic adventure that spans six different stories: *The Ribos Operation*; *The Pirate Planet*; *The Stones of Blood*; *The Androids of Tara*; *The Power of Kroll*; *The Armageddon Factor*.

CITY OF DEATH

In Paris in 1979, Count Scarlioni is sponsoring dangerous time experiments. Working with a British private detective called Duggan, the Doctor discovers that Scarlioni is planning to steal the *Mona Lisa* from the Louvre. He has six more 'genuine' *Mona Lisa* paintings – all painted by Leonardo – and plans to sell all seven.

When the Doctor travels back to 1505 to see Leonardo, he meets Captain Tancredi – another 'aspect' of Scarlioni. They are both facets of an alien Jagaroth called Scaroth. When his spaceship exploded on prehistoric Earth, Scaroth was splintered through time. His various selves have been working to ensure that the furthest forward in time – Scarlioni – can travel back and save himself and his people from the explosion that killed them.

But that same explosion also started the process of life on Earth, so the Doctor, Romana and Duggan have to stop him . . .

City of Death was the first story to be filmed partly abroad – with scenes set and shot in Paris.

THE FOURTH DOCTOR'S COMPANIONS

BRIGADIER ALISTAIR GORDON LETHBRIDGE-STEWART

Helped the Doctor
In: Robot
Terror of the
Zygons
Played by: Nicholas
Courtney

The Brigadier managed to keep the newly regenerated Doctor busy investigating mysterious thefts. He later summoned him back to Earth using a space-time telegraph system, to assist against the threat of the Zygons.

Actor Ian Marter previously appeared in the Third Doctor story *Carnival of Monsters*, and before that was considered for the role of Captain Mike Yates.

SARAH JANE SMITH

Helped the Doctor
From: The Time Warrior
Until: The Hand of Fear
Played by: Elisabeth Sladen

Having seen the Doctor change into a new person, Sarah soon came to terms with the concept of regeneration and was one of the Fourth Doctor's best friends. She travelled with him until she was forced to leave the TARDIS when the Doctor was apparently recalled to Gallifrey. The Doctor promised not to forget her – and years and regenerations later they did indeed meet again . . .

HARRY SULLIVAN

Helped the Doctor
From: Robot
Until: Terror of the Zygons
And: The Android Invasion
Played by: Ian Marter

Surgeon Lieutenant Harry Sullivan was seconded from the Royal Navy to become UNIT's medical officer. He was responsible for looking after the Doctor following his regeneration. Harry found the Doctor a rather difficult and unhelpful patient. When Harry expressed scepticism about the TARDIS actually being a vehicle, the Doctor ushered him inside to see for himself . . .

For several stories – *The Creature from the Pit, Nightmare of Eden* and *The Horns of Nimon* – K-9 had a different voice (provided by David Brierley in place of John Leeson). This was explained by him having had robot laryngitis in *Destiny of the Daleks.*

K-9
Helped the Doctor
From: *The Invisible Enemy*
Until: *Warriors' Gate*
Voiced by: John Leeson (and David Brierley)

A robot 'dog' built by Professor Marius to compensate for the fact he was not allowed to take a real dog into space with him. Due to return to Earth again, Marius gave K-9 to the Doctor and Leela after the robot helped them defeat a deadly intelligent virus swarm. The original K-9 stayed with Leela on Gallifrey, but the Doctor had already built K-9 Mark II. This second K-9 later stayed with Romana.

The motorised K-9 prop often broke down. There was also a lightweight 'dummy' version of K-9 for when he needed to be carried by someone.

LEELA
Helped the Doctor
From: *The Face of Evil*
Until: *The Invasion of Time*
Played by: Louise Jameson

A warrior of the Sevateem tribe, Leela was a huntress adept at tracking and killing. She helped the Doctor to uncover the truth about her tribe and about the 'god' Xoanon that seemed to have the same face as the Doctor. But when he tried to say goodbye, Leela ran into the TARDIS – and off on adventures. More than once the Doctor had to persuade her not to kill an enemy. She finally left the Doctor to stay on Gallifrey with Andred, commander of the Time Lords' Chancellery Guard.

ROMANA II
Helped the Doctor

From: *Destiny of the Daleks*
Until: *Warriors' Gate*
Played by: *Lalla Ward*

After recovering the Key to Time, Romana regenerated. It isn't clear what caused this, but after 'trying on' several possible new bodies, Romana settled on the form of Princess Astra of Atrios. The 'new' Romana's character was very different from that of Astra though – and more playful and humorous than her original self. She finally left the Doctor to explore another universe and help its people rather than return to Gallifrey.

ROMANA I
Helped the Doctor

From: *The Ribos Operation*
Until: *The Armageddon Factor*
Played by: *Mary Tamm*

Romana was sent by the White Guardian – disguised as the Time Lord President – to help the Doctor and K-9 recover the six segments of the Key to Time. Having graduated from the Academy with a triple first, she was at first rather scathing of the Doctor's qualifications and methods. But she soon came to realise that his experience and expertise went deeper than it appeared.

ADRIC

Helped the Doctor

From:	*Full Circle*
Until:	*Earthshock*
Played by:	*Matthew Waterhouse*

A boy from the planet Alzarius, Adric stowed away on board the TARDIS. He was a mathematical genius.

NYSSA

Helped the Doctor

From:	*The Keeper of Traken*
Until:	*Terminus*
Played by:	*Sarah Sutton*

Daughter of Consul Tremas of Traken, Nyssa travelled with the Doctor after her father was killed by the Master, who also regenerated into Tremas's body.

TEGAN

Helped the Doctor

From:	*Logopolis*
Until:	*Resurrection of the Daleks*
Played by:	*Janet Fielding*

An Australian air stewardess, Tegan entered the TARDIS, believing it to be a real police box, when she needed help with a broken-down car.

Too short to be an air hostess, Janet Fielding persuaded *Doctor Who* producer John Nathan-Turner that the height requirement for the job was lower in Australia.

THE FOURTH DOCTOR'S FOES

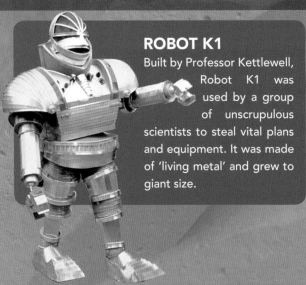

ROBOT K1

Built by Professor Kettlewell, Robot K1 was used by a group of unscrupulous scientists to steal vital plans and equipment. It was made of 'living metal' and grew to giant size.

DALEKS

The Fourth Doctor was sent by the Time Lords to prevent the creation of the Daleks on their planet Skaro, but he did not succeed. Later, the Doctor inadvertently returned to Skaro where he found the Daleks at war with the Movellans – a race of robots.

WIRRN

A Wirrn queen laid eggs inside one of the cryogenic sleepers on Space Station Nerva. The emerging Wirrn inherited human knowledge and tried to take over Nerva.

KRAALS

The Kraals created a copy of the English village of Devesham and the nearby space defence station as a training-ground for their android copies of the villagers and station staff prior to a planned invasion.

DAVROS

A crippled and mutated Kaled scientist, Davros was desperate for his race to survive the mutations caused by a thousand years of war against the Thals. His solution was to genetically re-engineer the resulting Kaled mutants, removing all emotions except hate and the instinct for self-preservation. He designed an armoured travel machine for the creatures based on his own mobile life-support systems – the Dalek.

SONTARANS

Still fighting their ancient war against the Rutans, a Sontaran assessment survey experimented on humans on a future, abandoned Earth. A group of Sontaran Special Space Service even went so far as to invade the Time Lord planet Gallifrey.

MORBIUS

A Time Lord war criminal, Morbius led a rebellion but was defeated and executed. Solon managed to save the brain of Morbius, and secretly built a new body for it – all he needed was a head. And the Doctor's looked ideal.

CYBERMEN

A group of Cybermen that survived the Cyber War against humanity tried to destroy Voga, the fabled Planet of Gold, as the metal is poisonous to them. They were destroyed by a Vogan missile.

ANTI-MATTER

This creature was a being composed of pure anti-matter energy that attacked visitors to Zeta Minor, the planet on the edge of the known universe. The Doctor struggled to persuade a group of scientists and soldiers not to remove the deadly anti-matter from the planet.

Although one of the best-remembered *Doctor Who* monsters, the Zygons appeared in only one classic *Doctor Who* story.

SUTEKH & MUMMIES

Ancient Egyptian mythology is based on the wars of the Osirans, who defeated the criminal Sutekh in ancient Egypt. Sutekh was imprisoned beneath a pyramid on Mars, but used robot Mummies to try to engineer his escape.

ZYGONS

After their planet was destroyed, a group of Zygons stranded in a damaged spaceship beneath the waters of Loch Ness decided to make Earth the new Zygon homeworld. They attacked using a powerful cyborg creature called the Skarasen – the Loch Ness Monster.

KRYNOID

A carnivorous form of alien plant life, the Krynoid can infect people, turning them into plants, and can channel its abilities into other plant life. Millionaire botanist Harrison Chase tried to cultivate the Krynoid – with disastrous results.

MANDRAGORA HELIX

A space-whirlpool of pure energy, the Mandragora Helix saw humans as a potential threat in the 15th century, and tried to assassinate the greatest Renaissance thinkers in Italy.

THE MASTER

An emaciated cadaverous figure at the end of his regeneration cycle and close to death, the Master tried to frame the Doctor for the assassination of the Time Lord President. He was later able to use the energy of the Keeper of Traken to steal a new body for himself.

ELDRAD

War criminal from the planet Kastria, Eldrad was executed by obliteration. But his hand survived and was able to influence people, including Sarah, so that Eldrad could reconstitute himself.

XOANON

When the Doctor repaired a spaceship's supercomputer, he accidentally left part of his brain pattern behind. The computer, Xoanon, became delusional, thinking it was the Doctor.

ROBOTS OF DEATH

Modified by mad scientist Taren Capel, the robot crew of a sandminer became homicidal. The Doctor and Leela worked with robot detective D84 to uncover the culprit and destroy the rogue robots.

THE FENDAHL

The Fendahl was death itself, draining life energy from its victims. A gestalt creature – a group entity – it was composed of twelve hideous Fendahleen and a 'Core', a beautiful female mutated from a human scientist. The Fendahl was so dangerous the Time Lords tried to destroy it.

THE ORACLE & SEERS

The ship's computer and its robot attendants saw themselves as god and seers on missing Minyan spaceship, the P7E.

VARDANS

A species that could travel along any broadcast wave, the Vardans were able to invade Gallifrey – preparing the way for a Sontaran force to arrive.

THE BLACK GUARDIAN

The antithesis of the White Guardian, the Black Guardian wanted the Key to Time so that he could wreak havoc on the universe and let chaos take hold. He employed a wraith-like creature called the Shadow to locate the final segment of the Key and wait for the Doctor to bring the other five segments to him.

THE COLLECTOR

The Collector was a Usurian who controlled all the human cities on Pluto and heavily taxed the citizens.

VIRUS SWARM

An intelligent virus swarm took over the crew of Titan Base, hoping to use it as a breeding-ground. The virus grew to giant size before the Doctor, Leela and their new friend K-9 destroyed it.

RUTAN

Sworn enemies of the Sontarans, the Rutan Host from the cold, icy planet Ruta 3 looks like a large glowing green jellyfish. The Doctor encountered a Rutan scout in an isolated lighthouse on Fang Rock in the early 20th century.

MAGNUS GREEL

A war criminal from the 51st century, Greel escaped in a crude time machine. He took a pig-brained robot called the Peking Homunculus with him to late Victorian London.

57

THE PIRATE CAPTAIN

The ruler of Zanak, the Captain promised a series of 'golden ages' to the inhabitants, and the planet's mines filled up with riches. In fact, Zanak was a hollow planet that the Captain materialised round smaller planets to mine their wealth. But the Captain was himself answerable to the ancient Queen Xanxia, who controlled the cybernetic parts of his body.

OGRI

A silicon life-form, the Ogri looked like standing stones – and several of them made up part of the stone circle The Nine Travellers. They were brought to Earth by escaped criminal Cessair of Diplos, and they fed on blood.

COUNT GRENDEL OF GRACHT

A nobleman of Tara, Grendel tried to usurp the throne from the rightful heir Prince Reynhart using an android copy of Princess Strella as assassin – but Strella was herself a double of Romana.

GRAFF VYNDA-K

The deposed emperor of Levithia, the Graff planned to raise an army of mercenaries to retake his empire.

KROLL

A giant squid mutated by the Key to Time so that it grew to gigantic size.

MOVELLANS

A race of apparently beautiful humanoids who fought a war against the Daleks. But the Movellans were themselves ruthless killer robots.

SCAROTH

The last of the Jagaroth, Scaroth was splintered throughout Earth's history when his spaceship exploded in primordial times. He struggled to re-assemble himself and prevent the explosion that killed him, but the same explosion sparked the existence of life on Earth. One of Scaroth's 'selves' was Count Scarlioni who stole the *Mona Lisa*.

ERATO

Named 'the Creature' by the people of Chloris, Erato was a Tythonian ambassador sent to negotiate a trading agreement. But Lady Adrasta hurled the enormous blobby creature into a pit so that she could continue to control a monopoly in rare metal on Chloris.

MANDRELS

Savage creatures from the planet Eden, a group of Mandrels escaped from an electronic 'recording' of the planet and attacked the passengers of a crashed spaceliner.

NIMON

The Nimon are scavengers, moving from planet to planet through black holes.

FOAMASI

A reptilian race that waged war against the planet Argolis. After the war, the Foamasi government officially owned the whole of their planet but criminal factions remained.

MEGLOS

The last survivor of Zolfa-Thura, Meglos was a cactus-creature that took on the form of the Doctor to infiltrate the nearby planet Tigella.

MARSHMEN

The inhabitants of the planet Alzarius evolved rapidly through several forms – starting from spiders, they then became 'Marshmen' who rose from the planet's swamps to attack the survivors of a starliner crash.

THE THREE WHO RULE

The Three Who Rule were a group of vampires, the survivors of an ancient spaceship crash mutated by the Great Vampire – last survivor of a war between the Vampires and the Time Lords. The Three – King Zargo, Queen Camilla and Counsellor Aukon – kept the local population in thrall, feeding on the blood of unfortunate villagers.

THARILS

A race of leonine mesomorphs, the Tharils once ruled a vast empire, staying safe within their Gateway between universes. But their slaves rebelled, creating Gundan robot warriors that could travel through the deadly time winds to attack the Gateway.

LOGOPOLIS

The Doctor decides to fix the Chameleon Circuit that disguises the TARDIS – and which hasn't worked properly since he left Totter's Yard in 1963. But the recently rejuvenated Master has other ideas. Together with Adric, Nyssa of Traken and air hostess Tegan, the Doctor finds himself on Logopolis, where the Logopolitans can control form and matter through the power of mathematics. Using Block Transfer Computation, they are also keeping the universe stable and warding off the effects of entropy – the heat-death of the universe.

But the Master does not realise this, and sabotages Logopolis. As Logopolis begins to collapse, the Doctor and the Master are forced into an uneasy alliance to try to stabilise the universe. At the Pharos Project on Earth, they manage to save creation, but the Master tries to turn events to his own benefit and hold the peoples of the universe to ransom. The Doctor defeats him – but falls from a huge radio telescope. The mysterious 'Watcher', an ethereal figure who has been observing the Doctor and helping his companions, blends with the dying Doctor to regenerate into a new body . . .

REGENERATION

The Fourth Doctor was once again a wanderer. He once told Sarah that he walks in eternity. After regaining his freedom to travel through space and time, the Third Doctor still used Earth and UNIT as a base – as his 'home'. But the Fourth Doctor soon left this behind. Once Sarah was gone, he rarely returned to 20th-century Earth, and when he did he made no effort to contact his old friends and colleagues.

His only Earthly companion after Sarah was Tegan – who joined the Fourth Doctor by accident in his final adventure, when his days were already numbered . . .

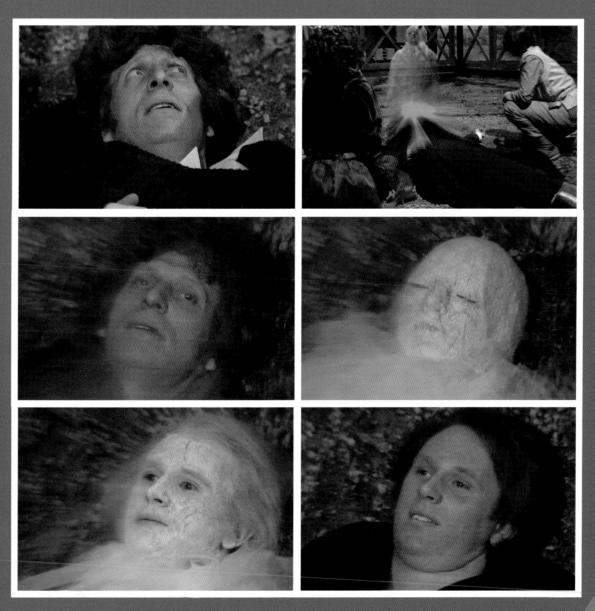

THE FIFTH
DOCTOR

Younger in appearance than any of the previous incarnations of the Doctor, the Fifth Doctor suffered more than his predecessors from his regeneration. He needed the stable, uncomplicated environment of the TARDIS Zero Room to recover. But he soon displayed the same wisdom and drive as his predecessors.

The Fifth Doctor was in many ways the most human and sympathetic Doctor so far. He became almost like the head of a family, his companions without exception having suffered loss – Tegan's aunt and Nyssa's father were both killed by the Master; Adric's brother was a victim of the Marshmen; Turlough was exiled from his planet and family; Peri was escaping from a dysfunctional family . . . The Fifth Doctor provided all these young people with a safe haven; a home. When things became too much for Tegan and she left, the Doctor was devastated by the thought that he had let her down.

WHO IS THE FIFTH DOCTOR?

Despite being only in his twenties (born in 1951), Peter Davison was an established and well-known television actor when he was cast as the Doctor. He was best known for playing the role of Tristan Farnon in *All Creatures Great and Small*. Initially reluctant to accept the role, Davison took the advice of Second Doctor, Patrick Troughton, that three years was a good length of time to stay in the role, and left in 1984.

Since his time as the Doctor, Peter Davison has continued to work extensively, particularly on television, and returned to the role for a short Children in Need *Doctor Who* special, *Time Crash*, in 2007.

ADVENTURES IN SPACE AND TIME

KINDA

On the planet Deva Loka, home of the Kinda tribe, Tegan comes under the malign influence of the Mara – a creature from Kinda mythology that manifests itself in dreams and nightmares.

With the help of the Kinda, the Doctor traps Tegan inside a circle of mirrors, and the Mara leaves her. It becomes a giant snake which is banished back to the 'dark places' of the mind . . .

The appearance of the Cybermen at the end of Episode 1 of *Earthshock* was a real surprise to viewers, as there was no advance publicity about their return.

EARTHSHOCK

A group of security troopers is attacked by androids in an underground cave system. The Doctor helps them destroy the androids, and finds they were guarding a huge bomb designed to destroy a peace conference. The Doctor traces the control signals to a space freighter where hundreds of storage silos burst open to reveal Cybermen.

When the Doctor disarms the bomb, the Cybermen try to crash the freighter into the conference. But the freighter falls back through time and instead of destroying the conference, the crash causes the extinction of the dinosaurs. The Doctor's companion Adric is killed as he tries to prevent the crash . . .

MAWDRYN UNDEAD

The Doctor meets the Brigadier, now retired and teaching at a private school, in 1983. In 1977, Nyssa and Tegan meet a younger version of the Brigadier. The Doctor also meets schoolboy Turlough, without realising that he is an alien agent of the Black Guardian, with orders to kill the Doctor.

They all meet again on a spaceship where Mawdryn and his fellow mutants are imprisoned for stealing Time Lord technology to extend their lives. Now they wish only to die. The Doctor is forced to sacrifice his remaining regenerations to provide the energy to fulfil this ambition. But when two versions of the Brigadier from the different time zones meet, it provides the necessary energy instead.

THE FIVE DOCTORS

The first five Doctors are taken out of time and space and transported – along with several of their companions – to the Death Zone on Gallifrey. The Fourth Doctor is caught in the Time Vortex, but the others find themselves battling against hostile alien creatures including a Yeti, a Raston Warrior Robot, a Dalek, and a troop of Cybermen . . .

   The Time Lords send the Master to help, and everyone converges on the Dark Tower – Rassilon's tomb. It turns out that President Borusa has brought the Doctors here so that they can gain access to the tomb, as Borusa craves the gift of eternal life that Rassilon is said to hold.

RESURRECTION OF THE DALEKS

The Daleks attack a space station where Davros is held captive, and release him. They also bring the TARDIS to London in 1984 – where the Daleks have set up a time corridor to their ship.

   Davros tries to usurp the Dalek Supreme who sends loyal Daleks to exterminate him. Davros releases a virus deadly to the Daleks, and the Doctor also releases the virus in London – destroying the Daleks there.

ADRIC
Helped the Doctor
From: *Full Circle*
Until: *Earthshock*
Played by: *Matthew Waterhouse*

The name Adric is an anagram of 'Dirac' – the name of the eminent physicist who predicted the existence of anti-matter.

The young Alzarian Adric found himself rather out of place in the TARDIS. He was now travelling with a very different Doctor and two young women. But despite his occasional sulks and irritation, the TARDIS was the closest Adric had to a home. And despite their apparent indifference when he was alive, his friends were devastated by his death.

Nyssa was not originally intended to be a companion.

TEGAN JOVANKA
Helped the Doctor
From: *Logopolis*
Until: *Resurrection of the Daleks*
Played by: *Janet Fielding*

Forthright and outspoken, Tegan never chose to travel in the TARDIS. She was trapped after the Master killed her aunt Vanessa. But she was disappointed and sad when the Doctor accidentally left her behind at the end of *Time-Flight*. She met the Doctor again in Amsterdam soon afterwards, but finally decided to leave when she felt that TARDIS travel had stopped being fun.

NYSSA
Helped the Doctor
From: *The Keeper of Traken*
Until: *Terminus*
Played by: *Sarah Sutton*

The daughter of a nobleman, Nyssa always struggled a little with life on the TARDIS. She was more than capable in technical knowledge and practical ability – devising a way of destroying the Terileptil Android when it attacked. Deeply caring and sympathetic, Nyssa left to help find a cure for the people suffering from Lazar's Disease on Terminus.

TURLOUGH
Helped the Doctor

From:	*Mawdryn Undead*
Until:	*Planet of Fire*
Played by:	Mark Strickson

Expelled from his home planet Trion, Vislor Turlough was exiled to a private school on Earth, where one of his teachers was the retired Brigadier. The Black Guardian recruited Turlough to befriend and then assassinate the Doctor, but the boy was never comfortable in his double role. He finally broke free of the Black Guardian's control, and was eventually reunited with his brother and able to return home.

BRIGADIER ALISTAIR GORDON LETHBRIDGE-STEWART (RETIRED)
Helped the Doctor

In:	*Mawdryn Undead*
	The Five Doctors
Played by:	Nicholas Courtney

After retiring from UNIT, the Brigadier taught maths at a private school. The shock of meeting his future self after being reunited with the Doctor gave him a nervous breakdown and partial amnesia.

Kamelion only appears in *The King's Demons* and *Planet of Fire*, though a scene with him in the TARDIS was shot for *Frontios* but not used.

KAMELION
Helped the Doctor

From:	*The King's Demons*
Until:	*Planet of Fire* (intermittently)

A shape-changing robot originally constructed as a weapon to help invade the planet Xeriphas, Kamelion was easily influenced by the hypnotic power of the Master.

PERI
Helped the Doctor

From:	*Planet of Fire*
Until:	*The Trial of a Time Lord*
Played by:	Nicola Bryant

American Perpugilliam Brown – Peri for short – was on holiday with her stepfather on Lanzarote when she got into trouble while swimming. Turlough rescued her and took her to the TARDIS to recover.

Actress Nicola Bryant, who played Peri, is not American.

THE FIFTH DOCTOR'S FOES

THE MASTER

Immediately after the Doctor had regenerated, the Master tried again to kill him. Throughout his fifth incarnation, the Doctor was beset by the Master, often in disguise, as the rogue Time Lord tried to get the upper hand. He 'stole' a Concorde aircraft and took it back in time, and subverted the Doctor's new companion, Kamelion.

THE MARA

A snake-like creature of the mind that inhabits the world of nightmares, the Mara possessed Tegan on the planet Deva Loka, and again on Manussa.

TERILEPTILS

Reptilian creatures with a love of beauty that belied their grotesque appearance. A group of escaped Terileptil criminals crashed in 17th-century England, and used a variation of the Black Death to try to gain control of Earth, but the Doctor destroyed the virus – inadvertently starting the Great Fire of London.

MONARCH

Ruler of the Urbankans, Monarch believed himself to be God. He resolved to travel faster than light to go back to the creation of the universe and meet himself. He was accompanied by humans placed into android bodies, and his ministers of Enlightenment and Persuasion.

OMEGA

Omega apparently survived the end of his anti-matter world (*The Three Doctors*), and tried to 'bond' with the Doctor to get a new physical body in the real universe.

THE BLACK GUARDIAN

The Black Guardian tried to destroy the Fifth Doctor several times, and recruited Turlough as an assassin. But Turlough was also to escape from the Black Guardian's influence by refusing the gift of 'Enlightenment'.

CYBERMEN

The Fifth Doctor encountered an army of Cybermen hidden on a freighter bound for Earth. The Cybermen planned to destroy a conference where an alliance against them was due to be agreed. When the Doctor thwarted their plans, they decided to crash the freighter into Earth.

MAWDRYN

A mutant humanoid, Mawdryn and his fellows used stolen Time Lord technology to extend their lives. But they were trapped in an everlasting cycle of ageing and suffering.

ETERNALS

A race that existed outside of time, the Eternals kidnapped humans and forced them to race giant space sailing-ships across the solar system to alleviate their unending boredom.

SILURIANS & SEA DEVILS

A group of Silurians and Sea Devil warriors attacked the underwater Seabase 4 in an attempt to set off a nuclear war on future Earth. They used the Myrka – an armoured, electrified sea creature – to breach the base's defences.

THE MALUS

A living creature re-engineered as an instrument of war, the Malus lay dormant beneath the village church of Little Hodcombe until awakened by a re-enactment of a Civil War battle.

BORUSA

Now President of the Time Lords, Borusa ordered the execution of the Doctor to prevent Omega getting access to his body. Later, Borusa tried to gain the secret of eternal life, bringing together the first five Doctors to enter the Death Zone on Gallifrey and discover the secrets of the Tomb of Rassilon.

TRACTATORS

Creatures that can influence gravitational forces, the Tractators were led by the Gravis who tried to steal the TARDIS. They attacked the planet Frontios by dragging down meteorites from space to bombard the human colonists.

SHARAZ JEK

Horribly burned by molten mud, Sharaz Jek led a one-man rebellion against the industrialist Morgus, who engineered his 'accident'. Using androids, he held off government forces on Androzani Minor, and denied the population the Spectrox they craved to lengthen their lives. His price for peace was the head of Morgus.

THE DALEKS & DAVROS

The Daleks were losing their war against the Movellans, falling prey to a genetically engineered virus that attacked the Dalek creatures inside their casings. Davros had been frozen in a cryogenic chamber on a prison station for ninety years when the Daleks came to rescue him.

Sarah Jane Smith actress Elisabeth Sladen's husband, Brian Miller, appeared as Dugdale in *Snakedance*, and provided some of the Dalek voices in *Resurrection of the Daleks* and the Seventh Doctor adventure *Remembrance of the Daleks*.

Commander Maxil, responsible for executing the Doctor in *Arc of Infinity*, was played by future Sixth Doctor actor Colin Baker.

THE CAVES OF ANDROZANI

The Doctor and Peri arrive on the planet Androzani Minor, where they are captured by a military group fighting against Sharaz Jek and his android rebels. Betrayed by ruthless industrialist Morgus, Jek has been terribly scarred by scalding mud. He 'rescues' the Doctor and Peri – craving intelligent and beautiful company.

Jek doesn't realise that both the Doctor and Peri have been infected by raw Spectrox. In refined form, Spectrox can prolong life – which makes it very valuable. But in 'raw' form it is highly toxic, and the Doctor and Peri are dying.

Jek's insurrection has closed down Spectrox mining. Morgus is desperate to get the mining started again, and there is a battle between the army, mercenaries working for Morgus and Jek's androids. Jek and Morgus are both killed, but the Doctor manages to rescue Peri – and give her an antidote to the toxin: the milk of a queen bat.

There isn't enough of the antidote for the Doctor as well though, and he collapses – regenerating into his sixth form . . .

REGENERATION

With the return of many old enemies – notably the recurring menace of the Master – the Fifth Doctor's time harkened back to his earlier years. But there was a vigour and freshness to the era that drove it forward.

The Fifth Doctor himself was also an amalgamation of young and old – suddenly seeming wiser and more learned when he put on his spectacles, yet taking a childlike glee in exploration and discovery. When he explained things to his companions, he was at once both their teacher and an enthusiastic fellow pupil, taking every opportunity to learn what he could from everything around him. It's appropriate that he finally 'died' saving the life of one of his young friends.

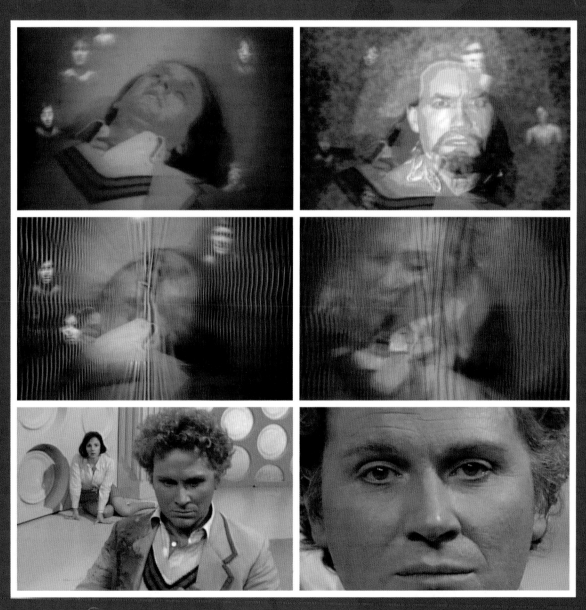

THE SIXTH
DOCTOR

The Sixth Doctor was larger than life in every way. Even the clothes he wore were extravagant and garish – a multi-coloured riot. He was loud and brash, and self-confident to the point of arrogance. It rarely seemed to occur to him that anyone else might have a useful thought or opinion.

But, like other Doctors, his brash exterior hid a softer, quieter core. Occasionally, we caught glimpses of the Doctor behind the showman. But whether he was loud and demonstrative, or more introspective, this was the same Doctor as ever.

He had a deep sense of justice and fairness and a passionate desire to see injustices corrected. Never was this more apparent than when he was put on trial by the Time Lords, and discovered that his own society was corrupt and rotten to the core.

WHO IS THE SIXTH DOCTOR?

The actor chosen to play the Sixth Doctor was Colin Baker. Uniquely, he had already appeared in *Doctor Who* – playing guard commander Maxil in the Fifth Doctor story *Arc of Infinity*.

Born in 1943, Colin Baker had been a well-known actor on television since the 1970s. He was probably best known for the role of the villainous Paul Merroney in the BBC series *The Brothers*, and also appeared as the even more villainous Bayban the Butcher in an episode of *Blake's 7*.

Although he only played the Doctor for a short time, Colin Baker is fondly remembered for the performance.

THE MARK OF THE RANI

The Rani, a renegade Time Lord scientist, is stealing a fluid from workers' brains in Killingworth in the mid-19th century. The fluid enables people to sleep – and, deprived of rest, the workers become rebellious and violent. The Master is also in Killingworth, seeing this as an opportunity to exploit.

   The Doctor works with inventor George Stephenson and local industrialist Lord Ravensworth to thwart the plans of the Rani and the Master.

THE TWO DOCTORS

The Second Doctor and Jamie are sent by the Time Lords to stop unauthorised time-travel experiments on Space Station Chimera. But the station's senior scientist, Dastari, is in league with the Sontarans. Together with the enhanced Androgum Chessene, they want to extract the Doctor's symbiotic nucleus – which enables him to operate the TARDIS – so they can complete the time experiments.

   The Sixth Doctor and Peri find the space station abandoned – except for Jamie, who escaped the Sontarans. They trace the missing Second Doctor to Spain, where they find he is being turned into an Androgum. Chessene and her colleague Shockeye turn on scientist Dastari and the Sontarans. The Doctor rescues himself before he turns completely Androgum, and Chessene dies attempting to escape.

REVELATION OF THE DALEKS

The Doctor has heard his old friend Stengos has died and is in Tranquil Repose, a cryogenic freezing facility on the planet Necros. The Great Healer in charge of the complex is actually Davros, who is turning suitable people – including Stengos – into a new race of Daleks. Those who are not suitable he 'recycles' as food for the starving millions of the galaxy. The Great Healer's business partner, Kara, plans to double-cross him and sends an assassin called Orcini to kill Davros.

Another of the staff of Tranquil Repose has also betrayed Davros – to the Daleks. The Dalek Supreme sends a task force from Skaro to take Davros prisoner. The Doctor and Orcini use a powerful bomb to destroy Davros's new army of Daleks, just as the Daleks of Skaro leave with Davros as their prisoner.

The 14-episode story, *The Trial of a Time Lord*, was actually made up of three 4-episode stories and a 2-part finale.

THE TRIAL OF A TIME LORD

The Doctor is transported out of time and brought to a space station by the Time Lords. Here they are holding an inquiry into the Doctor's activities – but when evidence is presented against the Doctor by the prosecuting Valeyard, it becomes the Doctor's trial.

The Valeyard claims the Doctor became involved in events on the planet Ravolox, and that his actions – apparently – led to the death of Peri on Thoros-Beta. But the Doctor suspects the evidence has been distorted and presents his own defence by showing events yet to take place on the spaceliner *Hyperion III*. With the intervention of the Master, for once apparently siding with the Doctor, the Valeyard is revealed as a villain, trying to take control of Gallifrey.

PERI

Helped the Doctor
From: *Planet of Fire*
Until: *The Trial of a Time Lord*
Played by: *Nicola Bryant*

Perpugilliam Brown was a botany student, holidaying in Lanzarote when she got caught up in the Doctor's adventures and whisked off to the planet Sarn. Her next trip took her to Androzani Minor, and ended with the Doctor regenerating into a very different persona. But despite a shaky start, the Sixth Doctor and Peri became firm friends. The Doctor was devastated when he thought she had been killed on Thoros-Beta, but it turned out that this was a ruse by the Valeyard and Peri had survived.

MEL

Helped the Doctor

From:	*The Trial of a Time Lord*
Until:	*Dragonfire*
Played by:	*Bonnie Langford*

How the Doctor and Melanie Bush met is not known – Mel was called as a witness at the Doctor's trial, and afterwards left with him in the TARDIS. Perhaps it is all part of a temporal paradox. Mel was with the Doctor when he regenerated into the Seventh Doctor, and finally left to try to keep the nefarious Sabalom Glitz in order and on the right side of the law.

Bonnie Langford was the first companion performer who was younger than the *Doctor Who* series, as she was born in 1964.

THE SIXTH DOCTOR'S FOES

SIL

A slug-like creature, Sil was the representative of the Galatron Mining Corporation on the planet Varos. His corrupt and unscrupulous business dealings helped to keep the people there in poverty. The Doctor encountered him again on his homeworld, Thoros-Beta.

Sil was originally intended to be 'swimming' in his tank of fluid, but that was too difficult to achieve – so instead he was sat on top of it.

MESTOR

Leader of the giant Gastropods that enslaved the people of Jaconda, Mestor was a slug-like creature that could exert great mental control.

THE RANI

A brilliant chemist, the Rani was a Time Lord who was exiled from Gallifrey when her experiments on mice turned them into monsters. She became the ruler of Miasimia Goria and later Lakertya, seeing the inhabitants as little more than subjects for her further experiments.

THE MASTER

Having thwarted the Master's attempt to take control of the leaders of the Industrial Revolution in England in the mid-19th century, the Doctor again encountered him at his own trial. The Master had been hiding within the Matrix – the sum total of all Time Lord knowledge – and revealed the truth of events to the Doctor.

SONTARANS

A group of Sontarans led by Group Marshal Stike attacked Space Station Chimera and captured the Second Doctor. They planned to learn the secret of time travel from him. But the Sixth Doctor realised his previous self was in danger and managed to rescue him.

CYBERMEN

The Cybermen stole a time machine and hoped to use it to prevent the destruction of their planet Mondas (shown in the First Doctor story *The Tenth Planet*). The Doctor travelled to Telos, and again defeated the Cyber Controller with the help of mercenary Lytton and the native Cryons.

THE DALEKS & DAVROS

Calling himself the Great Healer, Davros took control of the Tranquil Repose funerary facility on Necros. Here he used the cryogenically frozen bodies of humans to create a new race of Daleks. But the Daleks of Skaro discovered his plans and captured him.

It's implied that the Borad becomes the Loch Ness Monster – though the Fourth Doctor had already met a Loch Ness Monster in *Terror of the Zygons*.

THE BORAD

Ruler of the planet Karfel, the Borad was once a humanoid scientist called Megelen. But an experiment went wrong and he 'fused' with a hideous Morlox creature. Defeated by the Doctor, the Borad fell through a Timelash to Loch Ness.

Androgum Chessene was played by Jacqueline Pearce – well known for her role as the villainous Servalan in the BBC series *Blake's 7*.

ANDROGUMS

A life-form that believed in gratification and pleasure, Androgums were the servitors on Space Station Chimera. Scientist Dastari enhanced one Androgum – Chessene – making her super-intelligent, but she developed a craving for power.

VERVOIDS

A genetically engineered intelligent plant species, the Vervoids tried to take control of a spaceliner, the *Hyperion III*, before travelling to Earth. They viewed humans and other animal life as merely compost.

THE VALEYARD

The prosecutor at the Doctor's trial is in fact a version of the Doctor himself. The Master reveals that the Valeyard is an amalgamation of the darker sides of the Doctor's nature, somewhere between his twelfth and thirteenth regenerations. The Valeyard tries to destroy the Doctor and the Time Lords involved in his trial.

DRATHRO

An L3 robot left to maintain an underground survival system on the planet Ravolox.

THE END OF THE SIXTH DOCTOR

REGENERATION STORY

The first adventure for the Seventh Doctor, *Time and the Rani*, started with the TARDIS being bombarded by deadly rays. Inside, the Doctor lay unconscious. Then, as the Rani arrived in the TARDIS, the Sixth Doctor regenerated into the Seventh.

Like so much about the Sixth Doctor, it was unusual and unexpected . . .

REGENERATION

While he appeared in fewer stories than almost any other Doctor, the Sixth Doctor packed as much passion, emotion and vehemence into his time as any of the other Doctors. Perhaps by burning shorter, he burned brighter.

But beneath the veneer of bluster and the outrageous clothing lurked the same caring and intensely moral Doctor. His motives and aspirations were the same, if the way he went about achieving them was more obvious and outlandish.

We will never know how much time has elapsed between his fight against Davros on the planet Necros and his trial by the Time Lords, but it does seem that during that period the Doctor calmed down and mellowed. His relationship with Peri became less volatile and his swings of mood less pronounced. Perhaps if he had endured a little longer, his whole demeanour would have settled down into something more 'normal' – or as normal as the Doctor ever gets. But we shall never know.

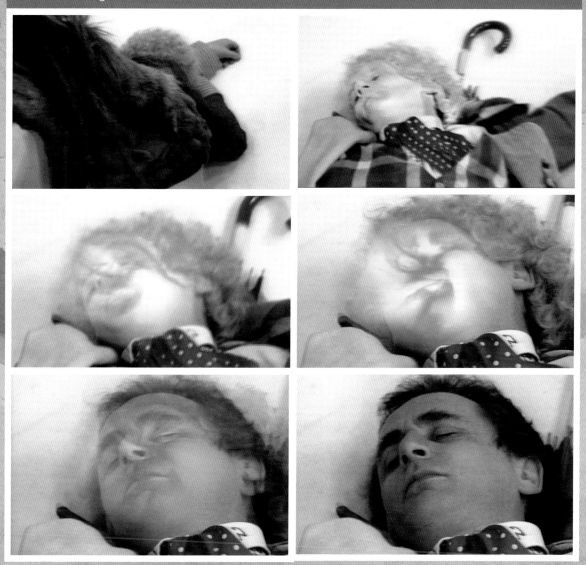

THE SEVENTH
DOCTOR

The Seventh Doctor was full of contradictions and paradoxes. In the same way that the Second Doctor often seemed to defeat his enemies almost by accident, so the Seventh Doctor came across as a bumbler and a clown. But again, beneath this buffoonery, there were glimpses of his deep intelligence.

While he seemed to stumble from one adventure to the next, the Seventh Doctor was also a master strategist. He planned ahead, working to an unseen but long-established agenda. His whole relationship with Ace was apparently based on his calculation that his ancient enemy, Fenric, would soon make his move in an epic game of chess where the Doctor had planned many moves ahead.

How much of the Seventh Doctor's advance planning was actually that – whether to play the game of Fenric, or to lure the Daleks or Cybermen into traps he engineered long ago – we shall never know. Perhaps it really was all just bluster, last-minute reactions and luck.

WHO IS THE SEVENTH DOCTOR?

Sylvester McCoy is the professional name of James Kent-Smith, who was born in 1943. After starting in the insurance industry, McCoy's acting career began as a ticket salesman at the Roundhouse Theatre, where he was spotted by director Ken Campbell. He was recruited to *The Ken Campbell Roadshow* (as a character called Sylvester McCoy), and later appeared regularly in the BBC children's programme *Vision On*.

After starring at the National Theatre in *The Pied Piper*, McCoy was offered the role of the Doctor. If you include the 1996 TV movie *Doctor Who*, he held the role for nine years – longer than any other actor. Since *Doctor Who*, McCoy has continued to act on stage and screen, recently appearing in the film *The Hobbit* as Radagast the Brown.

REMEMBRANCE OF THE DALEKS

The Doctor returns to London in 1963 to retrieve the Hand of Omega – a powerful Time Lord relic that can detonate stars. The Doctor left it here for safe-keeping, but now two rival factions of Daleks have tracked it down.

The Doctor does his best to stop the military (led by Group Captain Gilmore) from getting caught in the middle of the Daleks' battle. In fact, he has set a trap, and wants the Daleks to get the Hand of Omega. The Emperor Dalek – who turns out to be Davros – believes he is victorious over the renegade Dalek faction, but the Doctor has programmed the Hand of Omega to destroy the Dalek planet Skaro . . .

Time and the Rani and *Remembrance of the Daleks* both had pre-title sequences – the only stories to do this previously were Fifth Doctor stories *Castrovalva* and *The Five Doctors*.

SILVER NEMESIS

In 1638, the Doctor launched a statue of the villainous Lady Peinforte into space. The statue is made from validium – a living metal created as the ultimate defence for Gallifrey. In 1988, the statue returns to Earth, crashing down near Windsor.

Lady Peinforte travels forward in time to reclaim the statue, and a group of Cybermen also arrive to capture it. They are met by a force of neo-Nazis who intend to use the statue to establish a Fourth Reich. While Ace holds off the Cybermen, the Doctor gives the statue new instructions. When the Cybermen launch the statue to join their fleet, it explodes and the Cyber-fleet is destroyed.

Though *Dragonfire* was publicised as the 150th *Doctor Who* story, that counted *The Trial of a Time Lord* as separate stories. Therefore the honour actually goes to *Silver Nemesis* – which was also broadcast over the programme's twenty-fifth (silver) anniversary.

THE CURSE OF FENRIC

At a secret World War 2 military base, Dr Judson has invented the Ultima Machine to decrypt German ciphers. Base Commander Millington has located a source of deadly poison below the church and plans to use this against the enemy. As Russian troops arrive to try to steal the Ultima Machine, the Doctor realises from ancient local Viking legends that Fenric is about to be released.

Fenric is an ancient evil from the dawn of time. The Doctor defeated him centuries ago and imprisoned him in a flask. With vampiric Haemovores rising from the sea, the Doctor once again sets Fenric a chess problem. With Ace's help, he persuades the Ancient Haemovore – a powerful being brought back from the future – to turn against Fenric.

GHOST LIGHT

The Doctor takes Ace to Gabriel Chase – a house near where she lived. But in 1883 the house is owned by the mysterious Josiah Samuel Smith. It is a strange environment – complete with Smith's ward, a sinister housekeeper, a Neanderthal butler, a mad explorer, a visiting clergyman, a police inspector kept in a specimen drawer, and a stone spaceship in the cellar. There is also a creature known only as Control.

The Doctor realises that Smith is himself an alien – part of an experiment being run by the powerful Light, who Smith is keeping dormant inside the spaceship. The Doctor reawakens Light, who is seeking to catalogue all life-forms, but cannot cope with the concept of evolution.

MEL

Helped the Doctor
From: *The Trial of a*
                 Time Lord
Until: *Dragonfire*
Played by: *Bonnie*
                 Langford

Having tried – and largely failed – to put the Sixth Doctor on a diet and fitness regime, Mel found the Seventh Doctor to be a very different character. Nevertheless, they got on well and soon became friends. Mel finally left when she found someone else who could benefit from her 'improvement' regime – space rogue Sabalom Glitz.

ACE

Helped the Doctor

From:	*Dragonfire*
Until:	*Survival*
Played by:	Sophie Aldred

Real name Dorothy (surname never given), Ace was young and enthusiastic – especially about causing explosions. The Doctor met her on Iceworld, where she had arrived in a time-storm that was actually the work of Fenric. Ace was part of an elaborate trap Fenric had set for the Doctor, but he saw through it and helped Ace come to terms with her past and her own personality.

Sophie Aldred has done lots of voice-over work including 'appearing' in *Bob the Builder*, and as Dennis the Menace.

BRIGADIER ALISTAIR GORDON LETHBRIDGE-STEWART

Helped the Doctor

In:	*Battlefield*
Played by:	Nicholas Courtney

The Doctor and Ace met the Brigadier when he was called out of retirement to supervise UNIT's involvement in the events of *Battlefield*. The Brigadier risked his life to kill the Destroyer.

Battlefield marks the Brigadier's last appearance in *Doctor Who*, though he did return, with a knighthood, for a story in *The Sarah Jane Adventures* series – *Enemy of the Bane* – in 2008.

TETRAPS

A race of giant bats from the planet Tetrapyriarbus, Tetraps had four eyes – one on each side of their head, giving them all-round vision. The Rani used Tetraps to keep the people of Lakertya under control, but when she tried to leave the Tetraps behind on Lakertya to die when the planet was destroyed, they rebelled and captured the Rani in her TARDIS.

KROAGNON

Known as the Great Architect, Kroagnon refused to let people move into the city he designed as it would destroy the beauty of the place. His mind was trapped in the structure of Paradise Towers – until he found a new body . . .

GAVROK

Vicious and brutal leader of the Bannermen, Gavrok pursued the Chimeron Queen Delta to 1950s Earth where he tried to kill her.

KANE

Ruler of Iceworld on the planet Svartos, Kane was actually a criminal from Proamon, imprisoned there as punishment.

THE DALEKS & DAVROS

In 1963, the Doctor left the Hand of Omega on Earth as a trap for the Daleks. But it was traced by two rival factions of Daleks: 'renegade' grey Daleks that answered to the black Dalek Supreme, and white 'imperial' Daleks that were commanded by their Emperor. The Emperor turned out to be Davros.

CYBERMEN

A huge Cyber-fleet tracked the Nemesis statue to Earth in 1988. But these Cybermen seemed particularly vulnerable to gold, which poisoned them. They employed converted humanoids to prepare for their arrival, and tried to assassinate the Doctor.

THE KANDYMAN

Chief executioner on the planet Terra Alpha, the Kandyman is a robot apparently made of sweets.

THE GODS OF RAGNAROK

An ancient and powerful group of beings, the Gods of Ragnarok existed in two time zones: in their own temple, and also within the ruins of the same temple when the Psychic Circus performed on the site. They craved entertainment, and killed anyone whose act did not keep them interested.

THE DESTROYER

A demonic creature described as the Eater of Worlds and summoned by Morgaine to devour the Earth if her plans failed. She bound it with silver to do her bidding, but after she freed it to destroy the world, the Brigadier shot it dead with silver bullets – almost perishing himself.

LIGHT

A powerful creature that tried to survey all life in the universe. Its survey consisted of a creature that evolved through all possible life-forms, though Light himself was unable to cope with the concept of constant change and evolution.

FENRIC

A creature distilled from evil itself right back at the very beginning of time. The Doctor defeated Fenric at chess, and imprisoned him in a flask. But the flask was found by Viking explorers who brought it to Northern England, where it was again unearthed during the Second World War, and Fenric was released.

HAEMOVORES

Blood-dependent mutant creatures from a polluted future, brought back in time by Fenric. They infected or killed anyone they came into contact with. The Doctor finally defeated Fenric by turning the Ancient Haemovore against him.

CHEETAH PEOPLE

Feline inhabitants of a planet that was dying. The planet affected humans brought there by turning them into Cheetah people themselves. Even the Master was affected by its transformative power.

THE MASTER

Falling under the influence of the planet of the Cheetah people, the Master contrived to bring the Doctor to the planet to provide him with a means of escape. But after returning briefly to Perivale, the Master was again trapped on the dying planet . . .

THE END OF THE SEVENTH DOCTOR

BEFORE THE REGENERATION

After walking off into the distance at the end of *Survival* in December 1989, the Seventh Doctor would not be seen again until his regeneration in the TV movie *Doctor Who* – over six years later in May 1996. It would not be until March 2005 that *Doctor Who* returned to television as a series.

But during these 'wilderness years' the Doctor's fans were not starved of new adventures. *Doctor Who* continued – in the comic-strip adventures of *Doctor Who Magazine*, and also from 1991 in original full-length novels featuring the continuing adventures of the Seventh Doctor and Ace. Later, the novels would also embrace unseen adventures of past Doctors. From 1999, the Doctor also 'appeared' regularly in original audio adventures on CD, which are now available as downloads.

This wave of new fiction in different media continues to this day, with regular comic strips in *Doctor Who Magazine*, full-length prose fiction from both BBC Books and BBC Children's Books, and audio adventures from Big Finish. It's no wonder the Doctor got into the *Guinness Book of World Records* for the greatest number of novels written about a single fictional character, as well as holding the title for the Most Successful Science Fiction Series on TV.

REGENERATION

The Seventh Doctor became darker during his time. He went from buffoon to arch-planner, from someone who basically wings it to a person who has planned his every move for centuries in advance. Perhaps he was always like that, and it's just our perceptions and understanding that changed. Or perhaps, beneath it all, the role of the master strategist was itself an act.

Lady Peinforte hinted that there is more to the Doctor than anyone knows – a theme that will be picked up again, especially in the Doctor's Eleventh incarnation. As much as he has ever been – and ever will be – the Seventh Doctor is an enigma.

THE EIGHTH
DOCTOR

Although he only appeared in a single adventure – and shared his screen time in that with the Seventh Doctor – the Eighth Doctor was as fully defined as any of his incarnations. He amply demonstrated the same wit and intelligence and is, in many ways, the most 'human' Doctor of all.

For one thing, this is a Doctor who not only mentioned his own parents, but also claimed to be half-human on his mother's side. Whether there is any truth to this is unconfirmed, but the Master later seems to believe it.

Whatever his possible origins, the Eighth Doctor was every bit as driven and committed as his predecessors. He would stop at nothing to save the world – and displayed typical lateral thinking to achieve it. When he needed a police motorbike, he took the policeman's gun and then threatened not to shoot the policeman, but to shoot himself.

WHO IS THE EIGHTH DOCTOR?

Several actors were auditioned for the role of the Eighth Doctor, and the part eventually went to Paul McGann. Born in 1959, Paul McGann grew up in Liverpool with his three brothers, Joe, Mark and Stephen – all of whom are actors.

Paul was already an established screen actor, and had achieved cult fame when he appeared with Richard E. Grant in the film *Withnail and I*. Since playing the Eighth Doctor, McGann has continued to appear regularly in film and on television including, for example, guest roles in *Jonathan Creek* and *Luther*.

Daphne Ashbrook was the first American performer to be cast as a companion (Nicola Bryant, who played Peri, is from Surrey).

Grace was the first companion to be kissed by the Doctor!

GRACE HOLLOWAY
Helped the Doctor

In: *Doctor Who – The TV Movie*
Played by: *Daphne Ashbrook*

A senior cardiologist, Grace was called in to operate on the Seventh Doctor after he was shot in San Francisco. She was confused by his non-human anatomy, and the Doctor apparently died on the operating table. Not surprisingly, Grace had trouble accepting that the Eighth Doctor – who looked completely different – was the same man. But she soon came to understand just how extraordinary the Doctor is. Even so, she declined the Doctor's invitation to travel with him in the TARDIS.

THE EIGHTH DOCTOR'S FOE

A co-production between the BBC and Universal Television, the movie was shown by the Fox Network in the USA. But it was not successful enough there to warrant a follow-up series being made.

Eric Roberts, who played the Master, is the brother of actress Julia Roberts.

THE MASTER

Executed on Skaro by the Daleks, the Master's remains are placed in a casket and entrusted to the Doctor to return to Gallifrey. But the Master is resurrected as an amorphous blob of goo that escapes through the TARDIS keyhole. It takes on the form of a grotesque snake, and possesses Bruce, an ambulance driver. When this new body starts to decay, the Master is desperate to take the Doctor's regenerations to provide him with a permanent form.

The Master is finally sucked into the Eye of Harmony in the TARDIS – but is this really the end of the Doctor's greatest opponent?

THE NIGHT OF THE DOCTOR

The Doctor crashes on the planet Karn while trying to save the pilot of a damaged starship. He is revived by the Sisterhood of Karn and told that he is dying. The Doctor accepts his duty to finally fight in the Time War – the Last Great Time War, fought between Daleks and Time Lords. Drinking the Sisterhood's elixir and asking that his new self be 'a warrior', the Doctor gives in to his death, and changes once again . . .

REGENERATION

The Eighth Doctor's regeneration was perhaps the one over which he had most control, thanks to the Sisterhood of Karn and their elixir. He embraced death, and was a very different person from when we first saw him, his appearance and outlook clearly tarnished by war.

But he was still fuelled by a desire to save people, and though he chose to become a warrior, he died trying to save an innocent life in a war he wanted no part of. His last words were: 'Physician, heal thyself.'

THE WAR
DOCTOR

In some ways the most mysterious of all of his faces, this incarnation of the Doctor, who fought in the Time War, is the one we had the least time to get to know. Although he was disowned by his future selves, and himself discarded the name 'Doctor', this version of the Time Lord was still undeniably the Doctor.

This Doctor fought in the Time War for all of his life, and by the time he reached the end he was an old man, irritable and disapproving of the affectations of the young – though he still had a mischievous twinkle in his eye. This Doctor was born to be a warrior, yet at heart he was still a man of peace. He was understanding, caring, surprisingly polite and unwaveringly kind.

When preparing to destroy Daleks and Time Lords alike to end the Time War, the War Doctor took the weapon that would kill them all far away enough from his TARDIS so that she wouldn't see, and then complained at the lack of a 'big red button'. He believed that total destruction of both sides was the only option to finally end the war, and he committed to take the terrible guilt on himself. But when his other selves presented him with another way, he embraced it wholeheartedly.

WHO IS THE WAR DOCTOR?

Veteran actor John Hurt was already a giant of stage and screen when he was cast as the War Doctor for 2013's anniversary special. Born in Derbyshire in 1940, Hurt trained at RADA and swiftly won acclaim in film, theatre and television. His best-known roles were as the title characters in *The Naked Civil Servant* and *The Elephant Man*, but Hurt also appeared in science fiction and fantasy classics, including *Alien*, *1984* and the Harry Potter series. Hurt was knighted in 2015 for services to drama, and died in 2017.

WAR

THE DAY OF THE DOCTOR

At the end of the Last Great Time War, as the Daleks launch their final all-out assault against the planet Gallifrey, the War Doctor prepares to end things by wiping out Daleks and Time Lords alike. He steals the Moment, an ancient weapon so powerful that it developed a conscience to sit in judgement over anyone that tried to use it, and prepares to destroy Gallifrey. The Moment instead offers him a choice – a chance to see what his actions will turn him into – and opens a portal to the Doctor's future.

Through the portal, the Doctor meets his Tenth and Eleventh incarnations in Elizabethan England. Together, the three Doctors discover a Zygon plot to invade the Earth nearly five hundred years in the future. The Zygons plan to use stasis cubes, Time Lord artworks that freeze a single moment of time, to hide in until Earth has developed enough for their liking, and then invade it. The Doctors travel forward to the 21st century and convince humans and Zygons to negotiate a mutually beneficial peace.

Returning to his own time and the Moment, the War Doctor prepares to destroy Gallifrey. His future selves travel back and join him, and the Eleventh Doctor formulates a plan to save Gallifrey by freezing it in a moment of time, like the stasis cubes, ensuring the Daleks destroy themselves in the crossfire. The Doctors, joined by all of their earlier selves, as well as one from their future, manage to save Gallifrey.

THE MOMENT

The Moment (nicknamed the Galaxy Eater) was an incredibly powerful weapon, and so sophisticated that it had a conscience. It appeared to the Doctor in a form from his own future, Rose Tyler, and called itself 'Bad Wolf girl'. The Moment convinced the Doctor to save Gallifrey rather than destroy it.

NOT THE ONE YOU WERE EXPECTING

The Eighth Doctor appeared in only one television adventure and when the show was brought back in 2005 there was a new incarnation of the Doctor in the TARDIS. For the 50th anniversary, the show introduced a secret incarnation of the Doctor: the War Doctor, who existed between the Eighth and Ninth Doctors. A special minisode, *The Night of the Doctor*, was released that showed how the Eighth Doctor had died and become the War Doctor. The War Doctor himself then starred alongside the Tenth and Eleventh Doctors in the anniversary special, *The Day of the Doctor*, which was actually broadcast during the Eleventh Doctor's tenure (between *The Name of the Doctor* and the Eleventh Doctor's final episode, *The Time of the Doctor*).

THE NINTH
DOCTOR

On the face of it, the Ninth Doctor was more human than his predecessors. He dressed without flamboyance and he spoke without affectation. This was not a Doctor who quoted or postured, but one who got on with things and described them as they are.

But he was also a very alien Doctor. The contrast made his otherworldliness seem more extreme. When his priorities or outlook differed from his companion Rose's, it was very obvious and it jarred. The Ninth Doctor was a mass of conflicts and paradoxes. He made light of danger and relished adventure. Yet he was also painfully conscious that he was the last of the Time Lords – and that it was he himself who brought the Last Great Time War to its devastating conclusion.

WHO IS THE NINTH DOCTOR?

Christopher Eccleston starred in Russell T Davies' drama *The Second Coming* and, intrigued and excited by the possibility of working with Davies again, suggested himself as a possible Doctor. Born in 1964 in Salford, Eccleston was already an established screen actor, well known for roles in *Cracker* and *Our Friends in the North* amongst other series, and for several high-profile films including *Elizabeth* and *Let Him Have It*. His casting as the Doctor demonstrated the BBC's commitment to the quality and success of the returning series.

Staying in the role for only a year, Eccleston has continued to appear regularly on television and in films, with roles for example in *Heroes* and *The Shadow Line*.

ROSE

Rose Tyler is attacked in the basement of the store where she works by plastic mannequins. They are Autons controlled by the Nestene Consciousness. A stranger rescues her, introducing himself as the Doctor. Later he turns up at the flat Rose shares with her mum, Jackie – where he is attacked by a plastic arm detached from an Auton.

Together, the Doctor and Rose track down the Nestene Consciousness and rescue Rose's boyfriend Mickey. As Auton display dummies come to life all over Britain and smash their way out of shop windows, the Doctor manages to destroy the Nestene Consciousness with anti-plastic.

Despite Mickey's advice, Rose is unable to resist the chance to travel with the Doctor in the TARDIS . . .

In the Third Doctor story *Spearhead from Space*, the Autons were never actually seen to break through shop windows – it was all done by sound effects and clever editing. Russell T Davies wanted to remedy that for *Rose*.

THE UNQUIET DEAD

The Doctor brings Rose to Cardiff for Christmas Eve in 1869. Here they meet Charles Dickens, who is in the city to give a reading. But the theatre is suddenly alive with spectral creatures . . . The Doctor and Rose trace the 'source' of these to a dead woman who has walked out of Gabriel Sneed's funeral parlour – where the dead don't seem to stay dead.

With the help of Dickens, Sneed and servant girl Gwyneth, the Doctor and Rose discover that the dead are being possessed by an alien race. The Gelth have an affinity with gas. They claim they are looking for new bodies so their race can survive, and the Doctor offers to help them.

Gwyneth, who is psychic, creates a gateway for the Gelth to enter the real world. But the Gelth plan to kill everyone and live on within their dead bodies. Gwyneth sacrifices herself to close the gateway, leaving the Gelth stranded in their own dimension.

Simon Callow, who played Charles Dickens, reprised the role briefly in the Eleventh Doctor adventure *The Wedding of River Song*.

ALIENS OF LONDON/WORLD WAR THREE

The Doctor brings Rose home – and she discovers that she has been away, assumed missing, for a whole year. Jackie and Mickey are as distracted as everyone else when a spaceship crashes into the Thames. The pilot seems to be an upright pig, but the Doctor suspects there's more to it than it seems.

Sure enough, the Slitheen have infiltrated the government, and higher ranks of the police and armed forces, taking the place of key individuals. They plan to provoke a nuclear attack that will devastate the planet so they can sell off the remains as fuel.

The Doctor, Rose and Member of Parliament Harriet Jones are trapped inside 10 Downing Street. With only Jackie and Mickey to help them, the Doctor takes a terrible gamble that he hopes will destroy the Slitheen and save the planet.

Two Daleks were built for the episode *Dalek* – one battered and damaged, and the other in pristine condition for after the Dalek's 'regeneration'.

DALEK

Billionaire Henry van Statten collects alien artefacts in a huge complex deep beneath the deserts of Utah. One of his artefacts is an alien creature housed inside an armoured shell. When the Doctor arrives, he recognises the creature as a Dalek – and the Dalek recognises the Doctor. Absorbing energy from Rose, who has travelled in time, the Dalek returns to full strength. It escapes from its cell and sets about exterminating all humans – starting with van Statten's security troops.

But the Dalek has been affected by the energy it absorbed from Rose. Rather than live with the shame of not being 'pure' Dalek, the creature destroys itself.

FATHER'S DAY

The Doctor reluctantly agrees to take Rose back to the day in 1987 when her father Pete Tyler was killed by a car in a hit-and-run accident. Rose is unable to stand by and watch – and rushes out to save her father's life. The Reapers are creatures from outside time that take advantage of points in time and space where time itself has been damaged. They are drawn to the 'wound' created by Rose's actions, like bacteria. But unlike bacteria they sterilise the wound, which they do by destroying everything inside it.

Under siege with a wedding party in the local church, the Doctor hopes to use the TARDIS to heal the wound. But a Reaper consumes the Doctor. Pete sacrifices himself to put history back on track. He throws himself under the car that originally killed him, so restoring the Doctor and the other victims of the Reapers.

Writer of *The Empty Child*, Steven Moffat, was best known for writing comedy series such as *Coupling*.

THE EMPTY CHILD/THE DOCTOR DANCES

The Doctor and Rose search for a crashed spaceship in the London Blitz. They discover that children living rough on the streets are haunted by a strange, 'empty' child. At Albion Hospital, patients and staff have become lifeless zombie-like creatures with gas masks growing out of their faces.

Meeting mysterious ex-Time Agent Captain Jack Harkness, the Doctor and Rose discover the crashed ship was a Chula medical ship. The interior was filled with nanogenes, which leaked out after the crash and used the first human they found as a template from which to 'repair' all others. That human was the child Jamie – killed earlier in an air raid . . . Now the nanogenes are about to remodel the entire human race on a terrified child wearing a gas mask and searching for its mother, and equipped to fight as a Chula Warrior.

When Jamie is reunited with his mother, the nanogenes realise her DNA must carry the correct genetic information for humans, and the damage is corrected.

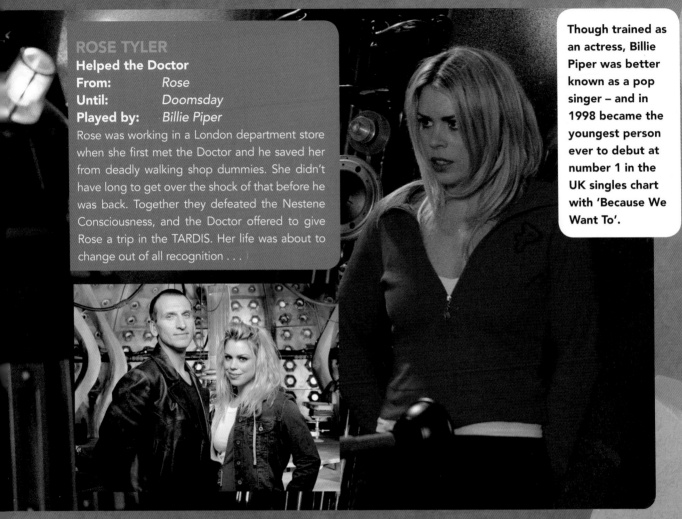

ROSE TYLER

Helped the Doctor
From: *Rose*
Until: *Doomsday*
Played by: *Billie Piper*

Rose was working in a London department store when she first met the Doctor and he saved her from deadly walking shop dummies. She didn't have long to get over the shock of that before he was back. Together they defeated the Nestene Consciousness, and the Doctor offered to give Rose a trip in the TARDIS. Her life was about to change out of all recognition . . .

Though trained as an actress, Billie Piper was better known as a pop singer – and in 1998 became the youngest person ever to debut at number 1 in the UK singles chart with 'Because We Want To'.

JACKIE TYLER

Helped the Doctor
In: *Rose*   *Aliens of London*
                 World War Three   *Father's Day*
                 The Parting of the Ways
Played by: *Camille Coduri*

Rose's mum, Jackie, didn't have a lot of time for the Doctor – not least as he took her daughter away for a whole year by mistake. It was not until she and Mickey found themselves battling against the Slitheen that Jackie began to appreciate him.

MICKEY SMITH

Helped the Doctor
In: *Rose*
Aliens of London
World War Three
Father's Day
Boom Town
The Parting of the Ways
Played by: *Noel Clarke*

Rose's boyfriend, Mickey, resented her friendship with the Doctor – and the fact that it led to him being suspected of murdering Rose! But when they fought off the Slitheen invasion, Mickey began to understand what Rose saw in the Doctor. The Ninth Doctor always called Mickey an idiot, but really he knew his true worth.

As well as a talented actor, Noel Clarke is a film writer and director.

ADAM MITCHELL

Helped the Doctor
In: *Dalek*
The Long Game
Played by: *Bruno Langley*

Adam was the companion who wasn't up to the job. The Doctor told him he only takes the best, and Adam failed to live up to that. Assistant to billionaire Henry van Statten, Adam was a brilliant young genius. After Van Statten's captive Dalek was defeated, the Doctor and Rose took Adam to Satellite Five, where he ignored the Doctor's warnings and advice and dangerously interfered with time. The Doctor took him home.

CAPTAIN JACK HARKNESS

Helped the Doctor
From: *The Empty Child*
Until: *The Parting of the Ways*
Played by: *John Barrowman*

A renegade Time Agent with a mysterious past, Captain Jack Harkness – or whatever his name really is – planned a con trick during the London Blitz. His actions had serious consequences, but after resolving the mystery of the 'Empty Child', Rose and the Doctor saved Captain Jack from certain death. He travelled with them until he was exterminated by the Daleks on the Game Station – but that was just the beginning of his adventures . . .

He might sound American, but versatile actor, singer and performer John Barrowman comes originally from Glasgow.

THE NINTH DOCTOR'S FOES

DALEKS

The Daleks that had survived the Last Great Time War were bronze-coloured metallic warriors. They had advanced hover capability, and their mid-sections could swivel independently of the rest of the casing. They were every bit as intelligent, clever, ruthlessly strategic – and deadly – as ever.

The 'voice' of the Nestene Consciousness was provided by actor Nicholas Briggs – who also provides voices for the Daleks and Cybermen as well as other creatures including the Judoon and Ice Warriors.

NESTENES & AUTONS

Its protein worlds destroyed and food stocks lost in the Last Great Time War, the Nestene Consciousness came to Earth – a planet rich in oil, smoke toxins and dioxins. For this third attempted invasion, it again used killer Autons disguised as shop dummies.

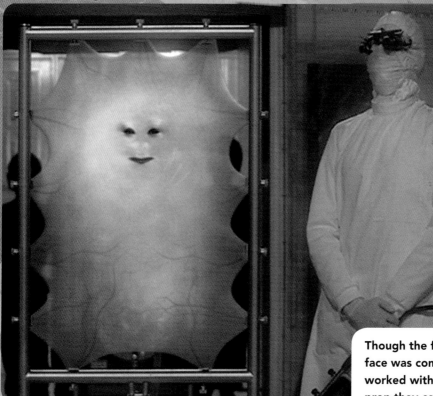

LADY CASSANDRA

The Lady Cassandra O'Brien Dot Delta Seventeen claimed to be the last surviving pure Earth-human. Rose wasn't convinced – Cassandra had had so many cosmetic operations that she had been reduced to a piece of skin stretched across a metal frame, her brain residing in a nutrient tank beneath. Her motives for witnessing the end of the world on Platform One were as mercenary as they were deadly.

Though the final effect of Cassandra's face was computer-generated, the actors worked with a 'stunt Cassandra' – a static prop they could react to and play off.

The Slitheen spaceship crashing into the clock tower that houses Big Ben was a mix of computer images – for the spaceship – and a model clock tower and spaceship wing.

SLITHEEN

A family from the planet Raxacoricofallapatorius, the Slitheen were dedicated to business above all else. They tried to turn the Earth into a vast stockpile of fuel to sell to the highest bidders. They could squeeze themselves into body suits so they looked human, and they augmented a pig so that UNIT believed it was an intelligent alien space pilot.

THE GELTH

An ethereal, gaseous race, the Gelth claimed to be nearing extinction. Their solution was to possess the bodies of the dead at Sneed's Undertakers in Victorian Cardiff. But they also had designs upon the living . . .

REAPERS

The Reapers were drawn to a wound in time – like the one created by Rose when she saved her father from being killed by a car. The Reapers tried to cleanse the wound – which in this case could destroy the world.

Originally, the Reapers were going to be cloaked humanoid figures with scythes – like the classic figure of Death.

THE EMPTY CHILD & GAS MASK ZOMBIES

The children living in the bombed-out London of the Blitz were haunted by a small child – a boy wearing a gas mask, searching constantly for his mother. He seemed to infect others, turning them into gas mask-wearing zombies. With the help of Rose and Captain Jack, the Doctor was able to unravel the mystery and save everyone, including the Empty Child.

JAGRAFESS

The Mighty Jagrafess of the Holy Hadrojassic Maxarodenfoe was an enormous creature that occupied Floor 500 of Satellite Five. Through its subordinate the Editor, it manipulated news reports – but who was it actually working for?

DALEK EMPEROR

Regarding itself as the God of All Daleks, the Dalek Emperor somehow survived the Last Great Time War. It waited patiently, building up a new army of Daleks until it was ready to attack humanity and destroy Earth. The Doctor was unable to defeat it – but Rose, drawing on the power of the Time Vortex itself, destroyed the Daleks.

Although many of the Daleks that appeared on their spaceship in *The Parting of the Ways* were computer generated, the Emperor Dalek was a model.

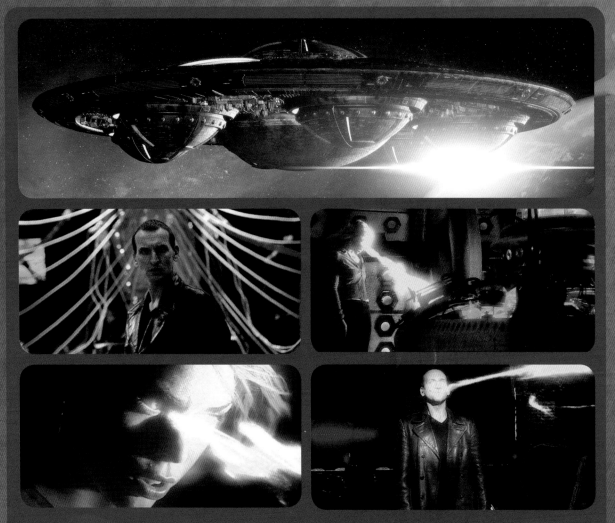

BAD WOLF/THE PARTING OF THE WAYS

The Doctor, Rose and Jack find themselves teleported aboard the Game Station where they are forced to take part in deadly game shows. The Doctor and Jack escape, but Rose is apparently killed. In fact she has again been teleported – to a Dalek spaceship.

For centuries, the Daleks have been manipulating humanity through the broadcasts from the Game Station, which is run by the Bad Wolf Corporation. A lone Dalek ship survived the Last Great Time War against the Time Lords, and they have been building a new Dalek race using humans harvested from the games.

The Doctor and Jack rescue Rose from the Dalek flagship – where the Dalek Emperor now believes himself to be the God of All Daleks. He orders the purification of Earth by fire.

The Doctor sends Rose back to her own time as he and Jack organise resistance on the Game Station. But Rose realises that the 'Bad Wolf' that she has seen and heard repeatedly is a clue, and that she can get back to the Doctor. During the process, she absorbs Time Vortex energy from the TARDIS, which enables her to destroy the Daleks – at the cost of her own life. The Doctor saves her by absorbing the Vortex energy, and regenerates into a new body . . .

REGENERATION

The Ninth Doctor was a troubled individual. When he first met Rose, he still felt the loss of his fellow Time Lords – a burden of grief made heavier by the knowledge that it was he who brought the Time War to an end.

But slowly, through his contact with Rose, the Doctor – like Van Statten's Dalek – became more human. Meeting Captain Jack further helped the Doctor's 'rehabilitation'. Finally, on the Game Station, the Doctor was unable to sacrifice all of humanity to destroy the Daleks – unable to take the same decision as he took before.

Again, he was saved by Rose who had absorbed the power of the Time Vortex. But the Doctor knew that same power would kill her. Having already saved all of time and space, it's fitting that the Ninth Doctor gave his 'life' to save his friend.

THE TENTH DOCTOR

The Tenth Doctor was one of extremes. For the most part he exhibited a joy of life that contrasted with the dark, more introspective moments of his predecessor. But his mood could turn in a moment. Faced with injustice or cruelty, the mild, witty façade dropped away to reveal someone who would offer no compromise; no second chances.

More than one of the Tenth Doctor's enemies underestimated him. For all his humour and evident love of humanity and tenderness towards his friends, the Tenth Doctor could be more dangerous and ruthless than any other.

But, unlike many of his opponents, the Doctor knew the depths of his capability. At times, he scared himself – and understood just how much he needed first Rose, and later Martha and Donna, to keep him in check. When he became human as John Smith on Earth in 1913, it was not because he was scared of what the Family of Blood would do if they found him. He was scared of what he himself would do to them.

WHO IS THE TENTH DOCTOR?

David Tennant grew up with *Doctor Who*. In fact, he has cited his love of the programme as one reason why he became an actor. Born in West Lothian in Scotland in 1971, Tennant's real name is David McDonald.

Already an established actor when he was given the part, the Tenth Doctor was just one role in a career that has encompassed stage, television and film. Tennant had already appeared in *Doctor Who* productions on audio and the internet. He is probably one of the UK's most well-known actors, and his performance as Hamlet for the RSC (while he was still appearing as the Doctor) cemented his reputation as one of the finest of his generation.

At the end of *Tooth and Claw*, Queen Victoria decides to set up an organisation to combat alien threats, naming it after the house in which she was attacked by the werewolf – Torchwood.

TOOTH AND CLAW

In 1879, the Doctor and Rose meet Queen Victoria as she is on her way to Balmoral. The Queen is forced to break her journey at Sir Robert MacLeish's house – Torchwood. She doesn't know that Sir Robert's wife is being held hostage by a group of warrior monks.

The monks are the followers of an alien life-form that has mapped itself onto the creature at the heart of werewolf legends. It plans to infect Queen Victoria and so gain control of the British Empire. Using the famous Koh-i-Noor diamond, the Doctor puts into operation a plan that Sir Robert's father and Queen Victoria's late husband Prince Albert devised to kill the beast using a specially designed giant telescope.

SCHOOL REUNION

Called in by Mickey, the Doctor and Rose go undercover at Deffry Vale High School. The Doctor becomes a supply teacher while Rose works as a dinner lady.

Sarah Jane Smith is also investigating the school and, with a repaired K-9, the team discover the head teacher and many of the staff are actually Krillitanes. They are cooking chips in Krillitane oil to enhance the abilities of the pupils to solve the so-called Skasis Paradigm. With that, Krillitanes will be able to control the very building blocks of time and space.

K-9 sacrifices himself to destroy the aliens. The Doctor again bids a sad farewell to Sarah. But he leaves her with a present – a repaired K-9.

THE GIRL IN THE FIREPLACE

A damaged spaceship has been repaired by clockwork repair androids. The Doctor discovers a fireplace that links the ship with 18th-century France. There are several similar 'time windows' on the ship – all of them connected to the life of Madame de Pompadour, nicknamed Reinette.

The Doctor meets Reinette several times during her life. He realises that the repair androids have used 'component parts' from the human crew to repair the ship, but still need a replacement 'brain' for the central computer. They believe that they can use Reinette's head.

The Doctor saves Reinette from the androids. But she dies tragically young. The TARDIS leaves – the Doctor never realising that the ship's name is *Mme de Pompadour*, which is why the androids thought her brain could replace the computer . . .

RISE OF THE CYBERMEN/THE AGE OF STEEL

The Doctor, Rose and Mickey arrive on a parallel Earth where Rose's father is still alive, but Rose herself has never been born. John Lumic, the owner and director of Cybus Industries, has plans to take his corporation's control beyond information and technology. The Doctor realises that in this world it is Lumic and his Cybus corporation that create the terrible Cybermen.

The Cybermen take over, gathering people at huge factories where they are turned into Cybermen. The Doctor confronts Lumic – now himself converted into the Cyber Controller – and uses the raw power of emotion to destroy the Cybermen.

THE IMPOSSIBLE PLANET/ THE SATAN PIT

On Sanctuary Base 6, the human crew and their servants, the Ood, are drilling in search of the power source that keeps the planet from being sucked into a black hole. But the planet is the ancient prison of the Beast and, if he wakes, the power that keeps the planet safe will end, so both prison and captive will be destroyed in the black hole.

The Beast begins to assert his influence over Ood and humans alike, and takes over the telepathic Ood, turning them against the humans. It also possesses archaeologist Toby Zed, planning to escape with him and the other humans when they leave Sanctuary Base. The Doctor finds the demonic form of the Beast chained up deep under the planet, and Rose ejects the possessed Toby out into space.

ARMY OF GHOSTS/DOOMSDAY

'Ghosts' appear all round the world – brought into existence by the Torchwood Institute. The Doctor tries to persuade Torchwood director Yvonne Hartman that her experiments are damaging the fabric of reality.

While Rose and Mickey investigate a mysterious Sphere, the ghosts materialise fully – as Cybermen. Then the Sphere opens to reveal it contains four Daleks, the legendary Cult of Skaro.

Millions of Cybermen come through the Void between realities, and suggest an alliance with the Daleks. But the Daleks see the Cybermen as pests to be exterminated. The Daleks easily exterminate the Cybermen, despite being vastly outnumbered. They open their Genesis Ark – a prison ship captured from the Time Lords – and hundreds of Daleks emerge in the skies over London. The Doctor re-opens the Void and the Daleks and Cybermen are sucked back into the empty space between universes.

But Rose is trapped in the other world when the Doctor is forced to close the holes between realities . . .

THE SHAKESPEARE CODE

The Doctor and Martha enjoy a play at the newly opened Globe Theatre. They meet Shakespeare, who is writing a sequel to his popular play *Love's Labour's Lost* – called *Love's Labour's Won*. But he has fallen under the influence of three witch-like Carrionites. The ancient Carrionites developed a science that was based on words instead of numbers, and which exploits the power of language itself. To others, it seems that the Carrionites are witches, who chant spells and use magic.

The Carrionites use Shakespeare's words, coupled with the shape of the Globe Theatre, to create a 'spell' that will release other Carrionites from the Deep Darkness. But the Doctor gets Shakespeare to rework the play's ending as it is performed, and the words of power are turned against the Carrionites.

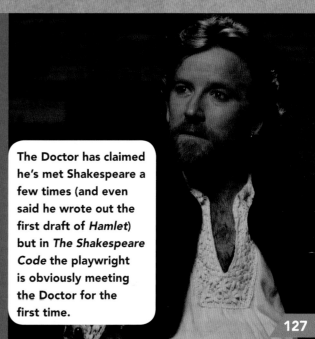

The Doctor has claimed he's met Shakespeare a few times (and even said he wrote out the first draft of *Hamlet*) but in *The Shakespeare Code* the playwright is obviously meeting the Doctor for the first time.

127

HUMAN NATURE/THE FAMILY OF BLOOD

The alien Family of Blood tracks the Doctor to Earth in 1913. They are after the Doctor's Time Lord 'essence' so that they can extend their short lives and live forever. Using Chameleon Arch technology, the Doctor becomes a human schoolteacher called John Smith. Only Martha knows the truth, and that the 'real' Doctor and his memories are hidden inside a pocket watch.

The Family track down the Doctor and animate scarecrows as their troops. John Smith – who has no idea that he doesn't really exist – has fallen in love with the school matron, Joan Redfern. He has to choose between love, or sacrificing everything to save himself and his friends.

Human Nature/The Family of Blood was based on a *Doctor Who* novel, also called *Human Nature* and written by Paul Cornell.

Elements of *Blink* were based on a *Doctor Who* short story (also by Steven Moffat) called *What I Did on My Christmas Holidays by Sally Sparrow.*

BLINK

Taking photographs in an old, deserted house, Sally Sparrow finds a warning from the Doctor written underneath the wallpaper. The Doctor and Martha are trapped in the 1960s – sent back there without the TARDIS by the touch of a Weeping Angel.

The Doctor has left other clues for Sally and her friend Larry Nightingale as well, including 'Easter Egg' messages on her DVDs. Following these clues, Sally and Larry evade the Weeping Angels, and find the TARDIS. They manage to send it back in time to rescue the Doctor and Martha. The Weeping Angels are left trapped – frozen to stone as they stand looking at each other.

UTOPIA/THE SOUND OF DRUMS/LAST OF THE TIME LORDS

The Doctor, Martha and Jack arrive at the very end of the universe on the planet Malcassairo, where human survivors have constructed a rocketship to take them in search of 'Utopia'. The project is led by the brilliant Professor Yana. But Yana is the Master – his personality hidden to escape the Time War. When the Doctor's arrival awakens his old personality, the Master regenerates, and steals the Doctor's TARDIS . . .

The Doctor, Martha and Jack get back to Earth to discover that new Prime Minister Harold Saxon is in fact the Master, who returned years earlier. 'Saxon' claims to have made contact with benevolent aliens and sets up a meeting with the 'Toclafane'.

But it's a trap and billions of Toclafane appear to take over Earth. For a year, the Master rules with the Toclafane – the future survivors of humanity. As he ages the Doctor into a small wizened creature, it is up to Martha to organise the people of Earth to defeat the Master . . .

THE SONTARAN STRATAGEM/ THE POISON SKY

Martha calls the Doctor (and Donna) back to Earth to help UNIT investigate Atmos – a navigation and anti-pollution system installed in most vehicles. The Sontarans are planning to use Atmos to emit a gas from millions of cars that would suffocate all humans but create the ideal conditions for Earth to become a Clone World.

Opposed by Sontaran shock troops, a cloned version of Martha, and by teenage genius Luke Rattigan, the Doctor adapts an Atmospheric Converter to burn off the deadly gas.

SILENCE IN THE LIBRARY/FOREST OF THE DEAD

The Doctor and Donna arrive in the Library – a vast complex that covers a planet – where they meet an expedition organised by Strackman Lux to discover why it is deserted. The Library computer, CAL, insists that everyone was saved, but the Doctor discovers the Library is infested with Vashta Nerada that hide in and imitate shadows, and strip the flesh from their victims in seconds.

CAL is actually the digitised mind of a little girl – Charlotte – and has 'saved' the missing people into the computer's own databank. The Doctor agrees with the Vashta Nerada to give them the run of the Library in return for allowing everyone to leave safely . . . But most of the expedition – including the enigmatic River Song – has been killed and live on only within the world simulated by CAL.

TURN LEFT

In the market of Shan Shen, Donna visits a fortune-teller, and her past life is altered by a Time Beetle – one of the mysterious Trickster's Brigade . . .

The Time Beetle latches on to a moment when Donna made a seemingly trivial but actually vital decision. She took a left turn in her car to go for a job interview that eventually led to her meeting the Doctor. The Time Beetle alters Donna's life history so that she turned right instead. This decision has far-reaching and terrible consequences. It means that Donna never met the Doctor, and without Donna's help, the Doctor died defeating the Empress of the Racnoss . . .

Without the Doctor, events he prevented actually take place. His friends sacrifice themselves to save the world in his place and put history back on track.

Midnight and *Turn Left* were made at the same time – so Donna appears only briefly in *Midnight*, while the Doctor is absent from most of *Turn Left*.

In some sequences of *Journey's End* where the Doctor meets his double, one Doctor was actually played by actor Colum Sanson-Regan (seen from behind!).

THE STOLEN EARTH/JOURNEY'S END

The Daleks have stolen Earth. They've transported 27 planets across space to the Medusa Cascade. These Daleks have been re-created by Davros, the Kaled scientist who first invented the Daleks on the planet Skaro. He has been saved from the Time War by Dalek Caan, one of the Cult of Skaro. Davros and the Daleks plan to use the powerful configuration of planets they have created to provide energy for the ultimate weapon – the Reality Bomb.

The Doctor and his many friends are captured. But a second Doctor is created when he is shot by a Dalek and his regenerative energy channelled into the hand severed in his fight with the Sycorax Leader (*The Christmas Invasion*). Caught up in the regeneration, Donna becomes part Time Lord, and manages to defeat the Daleks, but at a terrible cost. The Doctor is forced to wipe Donna's memories of him so that she can survive the otherwise fatal experience. With Davros and the Daleks defeated, the 'new' Doctor stays with Rose Tyler in the other universe where she now lives.

The Next Doctor was the last *Doctor Who* story to be shot on standard-definition video. From *Planet of the Dead*, *Doctor Who* has been made in the high-definition format (although an 'enhanced' hi-def version of *The Next Doctor* is available on Blu-Ray disc).

THE NEXT DOCTOR

Christmas 1851, and the Doctor is amazed to find another Doctor battling against the Cybermen and their Cybershades in London. But this other Doctor's sonic screwdriver is just a screwdriver, and his TARDIS is a hot-air balloon. He is a man called Jackson Lake who has absorbed the real Doctor's memories from Cyber-records.

The two Doctors join forces to defeat the Cybermen, who are using children as slaves to build a CyberKing – a massive mobile Cyber-factory.

THE TENTH DOCTOR'S COMPANIONS

ROSE TYLER

Helped the Doctor
From: Rose
Until: Doomsday
And: Turn Left   The Stolen Earth
Journey's End
Played by: Billie Piper

The Doctor gave up his ninth life for Rose, and she would have travelled with him forever. But, sadly, they were forced to part by circumstances beyond their control when Rose was trapped in a parallel universe, closed off from our own. However, as the Daleks once more threatened all of creation, Rose was able to get back to our universe and help the Doctor win the day.

JACKIE TYLER

Helped the Doctor
In: The Christmas Invasion   New Earth
Rise of the Cybermen   The Age of Steel
Love & Monsters   Army of Ghosts
Doomsday   Journey's End
The End of Time Part 2
Played by: Camille Coduri

On a parallel Earth, Rose's mother Jackie was converted into a Cyberman. But that was a different Jackie – the wife of a successful businessman, Rose's dad, Pete, who was still alive in this world. After defeating Daleks and Cybermen, the 'real' Jackie made her home on the parallel world with Rose and the alternate version of Pete Tyler.

MICKEY SMITH

Helped the Doctor
In: The Christmas Invasion   New Earth
School Reunion   The Girl in the Fireplace
Rise of the Cybermen   The Age of Steel
Army of Ghosts   Doomsday
Journey's End
Played by: Noel Clarke

Mickey got on much better with the Tenth Doctor than the Ninth. He even became a companion briefly. Mickey stayed on a parallel Earth after his counterpart there was killed by the Cybermen. But he returned to our world when the Cybermen tried to break through and invade.

SARAH JANE SMITH

Helped the Doctor
In: *School Reunion*
          The Stolen Earth
          Journey's End
Played by: Elisabeth Sladen

Sarah was working on a story about a suspicious school when she met the Doctor again. Even though he was in a different body, she soon found he was the same person underneath it all, and they renewed their friendship.

K-9

Helped the Doctor
In: *School Reunion*
          Journey's End
Voiced by: John Leeson

When the Doctor met Sarah again, he repaired K-9. But the robot dog sacrificed itself to destroy the Krillitanes. The Doctor was able to build another K-9 for Sarah.

> **The new K-9 that the Doctor gives Sarah at the end of *School Reunion* is actually K-9 Mark IV.**

PETE TYLER

Helped the Doctor
In: *Father's Day*
          Rise of the Cybermen
          The Age of Steel
          Doomsday
Played by: Shaun Dingwall

Rose's father was killed in a hit-and-run accident when she was a baby. But a version of Pete Tyler survived in another version of Earth – and was reunited with Rose and with Rose's mother Jackie.

DONNA NOBLE

Helped the Doctor

In:	*The Runaway Bride*
And from:	*Partners in Crime*
Until:	*Journey's End*
And:	*The End of Time*
Played by:	Catherine Tate

Donna was working as a temp when she got caught up in the plans of the Empress of the Racnoss, and found herself suddenly on the TARDIS. She helped the Doctor defeat the Racnoss, and later sought him out as she missed the excitement of adventuring with him. Fighting Davros and the Daleks, Donna bonded with the Doctor's 'spare' hand and became part Time Lord. To save her life, the Doctor had to erase all her memories of him.

MARTHA JONES

Helped the Doctor

From:	*Smith and Jones*	
Until:	*Last of the Time Lords*	
And:	*The Sontaran Stratagem*	*The Poison Sky*
	The Doctor's Daughter	*The Stolen Earth*
	Journey's End	*The End of Time Part 2*
Played by:	Freema Agyeman	

A medical student, Martha was transported to the moon along with her whole hospital and all the people in it. One of those people was the Doctor, who was pretending to be a patient. It was the start of a close friendship. In an alternate timeline, Martha travelled the world for a year, telling everyone about the Doctor. Finally she decided to leave the Doctor, and went to work for UNIT.

ASTRID PETH

Helped the Doctor

In:	*Voyage of the Damned*
Played by:	Kylie Minogue

> **Kylie Minogue was an actress before she turned to music.**

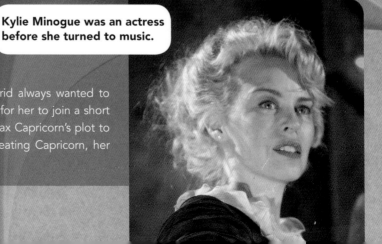

A waitress on board the starliner *Titanic*, Astrid always wanted to travel and see the stars. The Doctor arranged for her to join a short trip to Earth, and the two of them survived Max Capricorn's plot to destroy the *Titanic*. But Astrid was killed defeating Capricorn, her essence scattered out among the stars.

WILFRED MOTT

Helped the Doctor

In:	Voyage of the Damned	Partners in Crime	
	The Sontaran Stratagem	The Poison Sky	Turn Left
	The Stolen Earth	Journey's End	The End of Time

Played by: Bernard Cribbins

Donna's grandfather, Wilf became a firm friend of the Doctor and helped him when the Daleks invaded, and again when the Master returned from the dead. The Tenth Doctor gave up his life to save Wilf from radiation poisoning.

RIVER SONG

Helped the Doctor

| In: | Silence in the Library |
| | Forest of the Dead |

Played by: Alex Kingston

The Tenth Doctor had never met Professor River Song before she arrived at the Library. But she knew him – this might have been the Doctor's first meeting with her, but tragically it was to be River's last meeting with the Doctor . . .

JACKSON LAKE

Helped the Doctor

| In: | The Next Doctor |

Played by: David Morrissey

In London in 1851, the Doctor met another Doctor. Or so it seemed. But this Doctor was actually a man called Jackson Lake, who had absorbed information about the Doctor's life from a Cyberman info-stamp. He finally regained his memory, and together they defeated the Cybermen.

LADY CHRISTINA DE SOUZA

Helped the Doctor

| In: | Planet of the Dead |

Played by: Michelle Ryan

An aristocrat-turned-thief, Lady Christina was escaping from the police on a London bus when she met the Doctor. Moments later, the bus travelled through a wormhole to the planet San Helios. Lady Christina helped the Doctor get the bus and its passengers home again – before continuing her escape, this time in a flying bus.

ADELAIDE BROOKE

Helped the Doctor

| In: | The Waters of Mars |

Played by: Lindsay Duncan

The commander of Bowie Base One on Mars in 2059 when the Doctor visited. The base was attacked by an alien entity known as the Flood, and the crew infected. Though she was saved by the Doctor, she killed herself rather than let future history be changed by her survival.

ROBOFORMS

A robotic life-form, constantly in search of energy. They disguised themselves as Father Christmases to blend in during the festive season, and were controlled for a while by the Empress of the Racnoss.

> The Sycorax language is called Sycoraxic.

THE SYCORAX

A race of scavenger-warriors, the Sycorax used blood-control to try to blackmail the people of Earth into slavery. But the newly regenerated Doctor defeated the Sycorax Leader in single combat and saved the world.

KRILLITANES

A composite species, the Krillitanes could absorb the characteristics, and even the appearance, of races they defeated and conquered. The Doctor and Rose went undercover at a school to defeat a group of Krillitanes.

CLOCKWORK ROBOTS

Programmed to repair a damaged spaceship, the clockwork maintenance robots even used the crew themselves for spare parts. They opened time windows to the past to try to find Mme de Pompadour and use her head for the ship's main computer . . .

WEREWOLF

The Doctor and Rose encountered a werewolf in Scotland in the 19th century. It was actually an alien life-form that had modelled its existence on werewolf legends.

THE WIRE

The Wire was a criminal from another world who was denied a body by her own kind. She travelled to Earth as a bolt of lightning and took people over through their televisions, stealing their faces.

THE SISTERS OF PLENITUDE

A race of feline creatures that ran a hospital in New New York on New Earth. But they were creating specially grown humans and infecting them with diseases in an effort to find the cures.

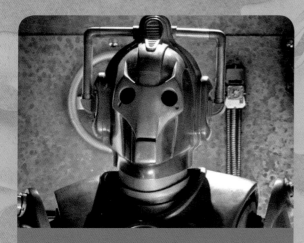

CYBERMEN

The Tenth Doctor witnessed an alternate creation of the Cybermen by industrialist John Lumic on another version of Earth. He also fought off an invasion by these alternate Cybermen, and defeated a group of them that created a CyberKing in 19th-century London.

THE OOD

From the Ood-Sphere, the Ood served humanity. They seemed happy to help, but were actually being exploited by unscrupulous humans. Telepathic, the Ood were susceptible to powerful minds – like the Beast, who took over the Ood on Sanctuary Base 6.

THE BEAST

The Beast was a powerful creature from before time itself began. It became the template for evil-incarnate across the universe, and was imprisoned on a planet circling a black hole.

ABZORBALOFF

A grotesque creature that could absorb people into itself just by touching them. Their faces remained visible as they were slowly absorbed.

THE DALEKS & DAVROS

The Tenth Doctor faced the Daleks on several occasions. He defeated the legendary Cult of Skaro, and defeated an invasion of Daleks created by Davros and led by the Dalek Supreme.

THE ISOLUS

Empathic beings of intense emotion, the Isolus looked like flowers drifting through space. A tiny Isolus child got lost on Earth in 2012 and the Doctor helped it back to its own people.

JUDOON

An intergalactic police force, the Judoon look like upright rhinoceroses. Amongst their other duties, they were responsible for security at the Shadow Proclamation.

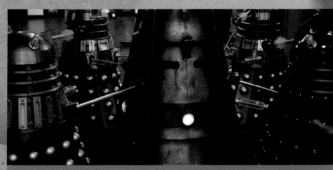

THE CULT OF SKARO

A group of four special Daleks charged by their Emperor to dare to think like the enemy, the Cult of Skaro survived the Time War in a void ship outside our universe. They even had names – Sec, Thay, Jast and Caan.

THE PLASMAVORE

The Doctor and Martha encountered a deadly Plasmavore, disguised as an old lady, at the Royal Hope Hospital. The Judoon quarantined the hospital – taking it to the moon.

RACNOSS

A race from the Dark Times, the Racnoss were born hungry and devoured everything – even whole planets. They were wiped out by the Fledgling Empires, but their Empress escaped.

CARRIONITES

The Carrionites were an ancient and powerful race from the Fourteen Stars of the Rexel Planetary Configuration. Their 'science' used the power of language instead of mathematics. To the uninitiated, this seemed like spells and witchcraft.

MACRA

Huge creatures, a bit like giant crabs, a group of Macra lived in the fumes beneath the motorway on New Earth.

THE FAMILY OF BLOOD

An alien family that took over the bodies of humans in their quest to find the Doctor. Short-lived, they wanted to steal his lives to prolong their own. They used molecular fringe animation to bring scarecrows to eerie life and attack the school where the Doctor worked as a teacher, in the guise of John Smith.

HUMAN–DALEK MUTANT

Dalek Sec, leader of the Cult of Skaro, bonded genetically with a human to become the first Human–Dalek Mutant. But he inherited some of the humanity, and the other members of the Cult of Skaro mutinied and exterminated him.

THE SUN-POSSESSED

Spaceship *Pentallian* used an illegal fusion scoop to take energy from a star. But the star the captain picked was an alien life-form which possessed the crew.

LAZARUS CREATURE

Professor Lazarus tried to change what it meant to be human. He manipulated his own metabolism at a genetic level to make himself younger – but the process turned him into a grotesque, savage creature.

WEEPING ANGELS

The Lonely Assassins, the so-called Weeping Angels absorb the potential time energy of their victims by sending them back in time. The Angels could only move when no one was watching them, otherwise they became stone statues.

FUTUREKIND

The mutated, savage remnants of the last vestiges of the human race.

MAX CAPRICORN

Founder of Max Capricorn Cruiseliners which owned the starliner *Titanic*. Capricorn tried to crash the ship to clean up on the insurance. He reprogrammed the robotic 'Heavenly Host' servants – which looked like classical angels – to make sure there were no survivors.

Harold Saxon – alias the Master – is the author of the book *Kiss Me, Kill Me*.

THE MASTER

Fleeing from the Time War, the Master used a Chameleon Arch to take on the identity of Professor Yana. But he reverted to being the Master, and stole the Doctor's TARDIS. On Earth, in the guise of Harold Saxon, he became Prime Minister of Great Britain, and used the Toclafane to invade.

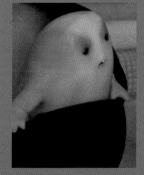

ADIPOSE

Creatures created from excess human fat. Miss Foster planned to absorb all human bodies to create more Adipose children, but the Doctor and Donna prevented this.

The Toclafane were based on an idea originally intended to replace the Dalek in the story *Dalek* if there were problems getting the rights agreed.

THE TOCLAFANE

Paradoxically brought back from the very end of time to invade Earth and enslave the human race, the Toclafane were in fact the final form of humanity. The Doctor and Martha were able to reverse the paradox so that the invasion never took place.

PYROVILES

Creatures of rock and fire. A group of Pyroviles fled to Earth when their planet Pyrovilia was 'lost'. Their destruction caused the eruption of Vesuvius.

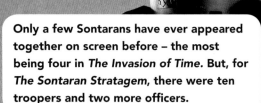

Only a few Sontarans have ever appeared together on screen before – the most being four in *The Invasion of Time*. But, for *The Sontaran Stratagem*, there were ten troopers and two more officers.

SONTARANS

The Sontarans tried to turn Earth into a new Clone World by poisoning the atmosphere. They also created a clone of Martha to help with their plans.

HATH

An amphibious race that worked with humans to terraform other worlds for colonisation. Like upright fish, they 'breathed' water through a mask.

VESPIFORM

From the Silfrax galaxy, the Vespiform were an ancient race. They looked like giant wasps, but could change their form.

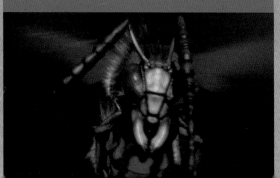

MIDNIGHT ENTITY

A formless creature that lived in the dangerous X-tonic sunlight of the planet Midnight. It tried to take over a tour group, which included the Doctor.

TIME BEETLE

One of the Trickster's Brigade, a Time Beetle tried to move history on to a different track when it latched on to Donna. In an alternate timeline, Donna never met the Doctor – so he was killed by the Empress of Racnoss and history was changed.

RASSILON

Legendary hero of the Time Lords and founder of Time Lord society. Rassilon also led the Time Lords in the Last Great Time War. But he tried to cheat extinction, using the Master as an 'escape route' for the Time Lords, and was driven mad in the process.

Rassilon has appeared in *Doctor Who* before – inside his own tomb in *The Five Doctors*.

STINGRAYS

Flying omnivorous creatures that consumed all life on the planet San Helios. They created a wormhole to travel to Earth but the Doctor stopped them – helped by the passengers of a number 200 bus and two Tritovores (a race which looked like giant upright flies).

THE FLOOD

A viral species that lived in water and took over anyone who came into contact with it.

CYBERKING

A huge Cyber-factory created out of the available technology in London in 1851. The Cybermen installed Miss Hartigan at its core, but she realised the error of her ways and the CyberKing was destroyed.

CYBERSHADES

Primitive, animalistic creatures created by the Cybermen in Victorian London to act as servants.

VASHTA NERADA

The piranhas of the air, the Vashta Nerada hid in shadows. In fact, they *were* the shadows, and could tear the flesh from a living creature in an instant. The Doctor, Donna and River Song encountered a swarm of Vashta Nerada in the Library, where they lived in the wood pulp of paper rather than their natural habitat of a forest.

The Master is reconstituted from his ring and bio-data taken from his wife, Lucy Saxon. But the reborn Master is insane, flickering between life and death. He is captured by Joshua Naismith, a billionaire who has an alien 'Immortality Gate' he believes the Master can repair.

The Doctor tracks down the Master. But he is too late to stop the Master using the Gate to project versions of himself into every human being on Earth – everyone becomes the Master.

The Master's madness is a result of the Time Lords creating a link between the final days of the Last Great Time War and the present – so that they can escape the Time Lock that keeps them trapped on Gallifrey. They travel down the link, and use the Gate to manifest themselves on Earth. But Gallifrey and the horrors of the Time War will also escape . . . The Doctor and Master together close the link. The Master is pulled back into the Time War, along with the Time Lords, but the Time Lock is restored.

All seems well – but Wilf is trapped inside one of the Gate's booths, about to be killed by a flood of deadly radiation. To save Wilf, the Doctor takes his place. As the radiation destroys his body, he says farewell to many of his recent companions before he returns to the TARDIS and regenerates . . .

The Tenth Doctor seemed to form lasting friendships and attachments more than most of the other Doctors. While they moved on, this Doctor returned to his friends, or sometimes they returned to him. After the initial introspective coldness of his predecessor, the Doctor had thawed out and remembered what he enjoyed about life and travelling the universe of time and space.

Out of all of his incarnations, it is this Doctor who is desperate to see his friends one last time before he regenerates. It's no surprise that it is the Tenth who ends his life protesting: 'I don't want to go!'

THE ELEVENTH
DOCTOR

The Eleventh Doctor was always a mass of contradictions. Although incredibly old, he seemed very young. He was wise beyond belief, but could be incredibly naïve. He was sophisticated and learned, but lacked many basic social skills. Most of all, he cared deeply, and yet could be rude and insensitive, tactless and gauche. When he stayed with Craig Owens, we saw just how much he didn't 'get' humans.

To his enemies, these contradictions were even more marked. This was a Doctor who wouldn't flinch at the death of an opponent, but who deeply felt the loss of every friend. He might have come across as ineffectual and dithering, but this masked the determination and steel that was the downfall of even the most ruthless creatures.

Old, wise, clever. Young, enthusiastic, witty. Caring, emotional, introspective. Uncompromising, determined, ruthless. Whatever else he may have been, he was the Doctor.

WHO IS THE ELEVENTH DOCTOR?

Matt Smith is the actor who played the Eleventh Doctor. Born in 1982, Matt originally hoped to be a footballer. But an injury ruled this out, so he pursued another ambition and became an actor instead.

As well as appearing on stage, he has worked extensively on television. His first role was opposite Billie Piper in an adaptation of Philip Pullman's novel *The Ruby in the Smoke*. Since his final episode of *Doctor Who* in 2013, he has continued acting on both stage and screen.

THE ELEVENTH HOUR

The newly regenerated Eleventh Doctor crash-lands the TARDIS in the garden of little Amelia Pond, but then accidentally goes forward in time twelve years.

The Doctor's reappearance coincides with the escape of a shape-shifting alien called Prisoner Zero through a crack in Amy's bedroom wall – a crack in the fabric of the universe itself. Prisoner Zero's jailers, the Atraxi, will destroy Earth in order to prevent the prisoner's escape. With the help of Amy's friend, Rory Williams, the Doctor delivers Prisoner Zero to the Atraxi.

THE TIME OF ANGELS/FLESH AND STONE

The Doctor rescues River Song from a crashing spaceship – the *Byzantium*. In the ship's hold is a Weeping Angel and security images of it 'infect' Amy.

   The Doctor and his companions make a nightmare journey through the crashed ship. Finally the Doctor destroys the Angels by switching off the artificial gravity field so that they fall into a crack in space and time.

VINCENT AND THE DOCTOR

The Doctor is intrigued to see a monster at the window of a church in one of Van Gogh's paintings. What did Van Gogh see? The Doctor takes Amy back to Auvers-sur-Oise in 1890, to ask him. The creature is an invisible Krafayis, stranded on Earth and attacking the local population. Knowing the creature will be at the church when Van Gogh paints it, the Doctor and Amy corner the creature.

   They take Van Gogh – who is racked with self-doubt and depression – to the future to see the exhibition of his paintings.

THE PANDORICA OPENS/THE BIG BANG

An alliance of the Doctor's greatest enemies has set a trap for him. The Pandorica is a myth. It is said to contain a mighty warrior. In Roman Britain, the Doctor and Amy discover the Pandorica underneath Stonehenge. They also meet Rory, who has returned as an Auton Roman centurion. Amy herself is part of the trap, but Auton-Rory kills her. The Doctor places Amy's body inside the Pandorica.

In the present day, with the universe ending because of a mysterious crack in reality, young Amy finds the Pandorica in a museum. Inside, her older self has recovered – and Rory is still waiting for her. Together with River Song, the Doctor, Amy and Rory manage to avert the end of the universe.

THE IMPOSSIBLE ASTRONAUT/DAY OF THE MOON

At Lake Silencio, a mysterious astronaut kills the Doctor. Devastated, Amy, Rory and River are astonished to meet an earlier Doctor. Travelling back to 1969, they all meet President Nixon, and the Doctor discovers that Earth has already been secretly invaded by the Silence – grotesque humanoid creatures that people forget as soon as they stop looking at them.

With the help of US agent Canton Delaware, the Doctor and his friends evade the Silence, though Amy is captured. The Doctor uses TV coverage of the Apollo 11 moon landing to implant a subliminal message in everyone to drive out the Silence.

A GOOD MAN GOES TO WAR

Amy and her new baby Melody Pond have been kidnapped. The Doctor and Rory hunt for them, and track the culprits to Demon's Run. Here, Madame Kovarian is gathering her troops and allies, including the notorious Headless Monks.

The Doctor also gathers his allies, and infiltrates the Demon's Run facility, where Kovarian is planning to 'program' baby Melody as a weapon whose target is the Doctor himself. As battle rages, Madame Kovarian escapes with baby Melody. Amy is distraught, but River Song reveals her true identity: she is Melody Pond – the daughter of Amy and Rory, which proves that baby Melody will survive.

CLOSING TIME

The Doctor meets up with Craig Owens, who he lodged with for a while (in *The Lodger*). With his wife Sophie away, Craig is looking after their baby, Alfie – with only the Doctor now to help. Meanwhile, people go missing from a local department store. In its basement, a dormant Cybership is coming back to life.

The Doctor, Craig and Alfie have to escape from a deadly Cybermat and find a way to stop the Cybermen from becoming active again. All before Sophie gets home.

THE WEDDING OF RIVER SONG

April 2011, and history is in a mess. Pterodactyls fly over London where Charles Dickens is still writing, Winston Churchill is the Holy Roman Emperor . . . Ancient and modern sit side-by-side, muddled together.

The Doctor is on the track of the Silence. He takes information from wherever and whoever he can – including a dying Dalek and the severed head of his old friend Dorium Maldovar. He also enlists the help of the shape-changing robot the Teselecta and its crew . . . He knows that 'Silence will fall when the question is asked'.

The Doctor explains to Churchill that River Song was the 'impossible astronaut' who shot him. Except she couldn't bring herself to do it. All history – all time – is at a standstill unless the Doctor dies and events unfold as they are supposed to.

Amy and Rory take the Doctor to the Great Pyramid in Cairo, where Silents are kept locked away and Madame Kovarian is a prisoner. But with the Silence breaking out of their containment and taking control again, and Madame Kovarian escaping from her bonds, the Doctor realises it is a trap. To force her to kill him, the Doctor marries River Song – and gives her a clue as to what will really happen if she disposes of him at Lake Silencio.

Events play out as they are supposed to, and the Impossible Astronaut shoots the Doctor, so that history returns to its proper path and the Silence are defeated. But all is not what it seems . . .

ASYLUM OF THE DALEKS

The Doctor is captured and taken to the Parliament of the Daleks, where he is reunited with Amy and Rory who have been kidnapped by Dalek agents. The Daleks want them to travel to the Dalek Asylum – a planet where mad and dangerous Daleks are confined. The Daleks have detected an unknown signal from the planet and want the Doctor to disable the defence shields so they can destroy the planet. It's that or be exterminated.

On the surface, they are contacted over the intercoms by trapped spaceship crash survivor Oswin Oswald. She can turn off the defence shields if the Doctor helps her escape, and alters the Dalek systems so that they have no knowledge of him. But when the Doctor finds her, a terrible truth awaits him.

Escaping back to the Dalek ship, the Doctor, Amy and Rory discover that the Daleks have all forgotten who the Doctor is.

A TOWN CALLED MERCY

The town of Mercy in Nevada in 1870 is under threat from a mysterious Gunslinger who won't let anyone leave. He demands the life of Kahler-Jex, an alien working as the local physician. The Doctor discovers that Jex actually created the Gunslinger. He was part of a scientific group that genetically and physically altered members of their own race, turning them into weapons.

The Gunslinger comes into Mercy to find Jex and kill anyone who gets in his way. But Jex sacrifices himself to save the town.

It might look like the Wild West, but *A Town Called Mercy* was actually shot in Spain.

The Angels Take Manhattan is Amy and Rory's last adventure with the Doctor, but the last adventure that was shot with them was *The Power of Three*.

THE ANGELS TAKE MANHATTAN

The Doctor, Amy and Rory are taking a break in New York when Rory finds himself plunged back in time to 1938. The Doctor is reading a book about 'Melody Malone' – a fictional 1930s detective – when he finds that Rory turns up in the story. The book seems to recount actual events.

In 1938, River Song – alias Melody Malone – has discovered New York is a centre for the Weeping Angels (including the Statue of Liberty). One of their victims is Rory – who meets himself as an old man. To break the chain of events, Rory and Amy jump off the roof of a building. It seems to work, and they wake up next to the TARDIS which landed in a graveyard.

But Rory finds his own gravestone – and while looking at it is touched by a surviving Angel. Despite the Doctor's warnings, Amy allows the Angel to touch her too. Reading the last page of the Melody Malone book – which was written in the past by Amy – the Doctor discovers that she and Rory survived.

THE SNOWMEN

The Doctor has retired. But in Victorian London, he encounters the sinister Doctor Walter Simeon, who is controlling snow – and homicidal snowmen. Possessed by the Great Intelligence, Simeon is keen to get hold of the reconstituted ice-body of a children's governess. The new governess, Clara, asks the Doctor for help.

The ice-governess comes to life, and the Doctor saves the children. But the governess and Clara fall from the cloud where the TARDIS is parked. As Clara dies, the raw emotion of the children and those who love her turn the falling snow to salt tears and the snow is banished.

The snow in *The Snowmen* – and most other 'snowy' adventures – was actually made mostly of paper.

COLD WAR

The Doctor and Clara find themselves on board the Soviet submarine *Firebird* in 1983, during the Cold War. Captain Zhukov's crew have recovered something from the Arctic ice – an Ice Warrior.

Thawed out, Grand Marshal Skaldak rampages through the submarine. The Doctor helps the crew to capture the creature, but the Ice Warrior's shell is merely armour and the actual Martian leaves it and escapes. With the submarine in danger of being destroyed, the Doctor struggles to convince the noble Martian warrior that the crew mean it no harm. If he fails, Skaldak will launch the submarine's nuclear missiles and trigger a world war that will kill billions . . .

Most effects in *Doctor Who* are now created digitally on computers. But the submarine in *Cold War* was an actual model.

JOURNEY TO THE CENTRE OF THE TARDIS

The TARDIS is caught in the grip of *The Hornet*, a salvage spaceship operated by the Van Baalen Brothers – Gregor and Bram, and their android assistant Tricky. The Doctor enlists the help of the Van Baalens to find Clara – who is trapped inside the damaged TARDIS. But the brothers see an opportunity to strip the TARDIS of its valuable components and make a huge profit.

The TARDIS fights back to defend itself from the 'salvage' operations – including creating 'zombie' versions of Clara and the Doctor. With Clara remembering things she shouldn't know, and the Doctor desperate to stop the TARDIS from exploding, they have to get to the heart of the TARDIS to avert disaster . . .

NIGHTMARE IN SILVER

Hedgewick's World is the biggest and best amusement park there will ever be. Except the Doctor's got his dates wrong, and so he and Clara arrive when the place is run-down and all but abandoned. It's a shame as they've brought the children Artie and Angie here for a fun time.

They meet a showman, Mr Webley, and a group of soldiers stationed on the planet. Webley shows off his prize exhibit – a chess-playing automaton: a Cyberman! Cybermen that survived the last great Cyber War have used the planet as a repair ground – kidnapping humans from the amusement park to provide 'spare' parts. Now the Cybermen are ready to rise from their hibernation tombs and wage a renewed war against humanity . . .

THE NAME OF THE DOCTOR

Madame Vastra is given the space-time coordinates of what is said to be the location of the Doctor's greatest secret. And it has been discovered. She convenes a 'dreamscape' meeting with Jenny, Strax, River Song – and Clara. Vastra also has a word – 'Trenzalore'.

The Doctor is horrified – knowing that Trenzalore is where he will be buried. When they arrive, there is a huge tomb. This will be the location of the Doctor's final confrontation with Doctor Simeon – the Great Intelligence – and his Whisper Men, deadly creatures which seem to be made of paper.

It is also where Clara discovers what the Doctor has been hiding from her – the fact that he has met her before, in different times and places. It is a mystery that will finally be resolved, and for the Doctor and Clara nothing will ever be the same again . . .

THE ELEVENTH DOCTOR'S COMPANIONS

Karen Gillan had appeared in *Doctor Who* before, playing one of the soothsayers in *The Fires of Pompeii*.

RORY WILLIAMS
Helped the Doctor
In:	*The Eleventh Hour*
And from:	*The Vampires of Venice*
Until:	*The Angels Take Manhattan*
Played by:	Arthur Darvill

Amy's friend from childhood, Rory always loved Amy – though it took her a while (and a nudge from their mutual friend Melody) to work that out. For a while Rory felt jealous of Amy's affection for the Doctor – she even went off with him the night before their wedding. But there was never any doubt of Rory's love for Amy – as an Auton he waited two thousand years for her.

AMY POND
Helped the Doctor
From:	*The Eleventh Hour*
Until:	*The Angels Take Manhattan*
Played by:	Karen Gillan

Amelia Jessica Pond was the Girl Who Waited. She first met the Doctor when he crashed the TARDIS into her garden, just after he regenerated into his eleventh incarnation. He said he'd come straight back for her, and Amy waited. She ended up waiting a long time for the Doctor to return, but she never forgot him – the Raggedy Doctor, mad man with a blue box.

RIVER SONG
**Helped the Doctor
In:**
The Time of Angels
Flesh and Stone
The Pandorica Opens
The Big Bang
The Impossible Astronaut
Day of the Moon
A Good Man Goes to War
Let's Kill Hitler
The Wedding of River Song
The Angels Take Manhattan
The Name of the Doctor
Played by: Alex Kingston

If River's relationship with the Doctor is a bit complicated, her relationship with Amy and Rory was even more strange. She has – perhaps – married the Doctor, but in a different timeline and he never completed the ceremony as he didn't tell her his name. Not then. But River was the child of Amy and Rory. So if the Doctor and River were married, the Doctor's companions would also have been his in-laws.

CRAIG OWENS
**Helped the Doctor
In:**
The Lodger
Closing Time
Played by: James Corden

Craig's rather ordinary life took a turn for the bizarre when the Doctor came to stay as his lodger. Later the Doctor returned – partly to help Craig babysit his son Alfie, but also to defeat a group of Cybermen hiding out below the local department store.

James Corden, who played Craig, is best known as a comedy actor.

IDRIS
Helped the Doctor
In: The Doctor's Wife
Played by: Suranne Jones

The Doctor gets a thought message from another Time Lord – the Corsair. He tracks the signal to an asteroid covered in junk within a small bubble universe. But the message turns out to be a trap. A strange being called House sent it, having already killed the Corsair and many other Time Lords. House transfers the TARDIS's essence into a woman. Disoriented, and calling herself Idris, she befriends the Doctor who gradually realises that she is his TARDIS. Amy and Rory are trapped aboard the TARDIS shell, which has been taken over by the mind of House. But the Doctor restores Idris to her 'home' as the TARDIS, and House is destroyed.

THE PATERNOSTER GANG
Helped the Doctor
In: A Good Man Goes to War
 The Snowmen
 The Crimson Horror
 The Name of the Doctor
Madame Vastra played by: Neve McIntosh
Jenny Flint played by: Catrin Stewart
Commander Strax played by: Dan Starkey

Madame Vastra was a Silurian awakened by work on the London Underground system. She became known as 'The Great Detective' and, together with her human wife, Jenny Flint, and her Sontaran 'man'-servant Strax, helped the Doctor on several occasions.

BRIAN WILLIAMS
Helped the Doctor
In: Dinosaurs on a Spaceship
 The Power of Three
Played by: Mark Williams

Rory's father was accidentally taken to a spaceship full of dinosaurs by the Doctor when he went to collect Amy and Rory. Later, he helped with the mystery of the strange cubes that appeared all over the world.

Mark Williams, who played Rory's dad Brian, also played the father of Ron Weasley in the Harry Potter films. But that doesn't make Rory and Ron brothers!

QUEEN NEFERTITI

Helped the Doctor

In: *Dinosaurs on a Spaceship*
Played by: Riann Steele

Queen of Ancient Egypt, Nefertiti and her people were rescued from a swarm of giant alien locusts by the Doctor. She then helped him avert disaster as a Silurian Ark Ship approached Earth.

JOHN RIDDELL

Helped the Doctor

In: *Dinosaurs on a Spaceship*
Played by: Rupert Graves

Charismatic but chauvinistic big-game hunter and adventurer, John Riddell was an old friend of the Doctor's even before the Doctor asked him to help with a crashing Silurian Ark Ship.

In the original script of *Dinosaurs on a Spaceship*, the Doctor knows that Riddell will die the day after he returns to Earth, but this plot strand was cut.

CLARA OSWALD

Helped the Doctor

In: Asylum of the Daleks
The Snowmen
And from: The Bells of St John
Until: Hell Bent
Played by: Jenna-Louise Coleman

To the Eleventh Doctor, Clara was an enigma and a paradox. The Doctor met her in several incarnations – in fact, Clara lived out many lives apart from the one in which she travelled with him. Down to earth, clever, and with a biting sarcastic wit, Clara had to come to terms with her paradoxical existence. She remained a great friend to the Eleventh Doctor to the last.

DALEKS

Cunning and ruthless as ever, a group of Daleks pretended they were war machines invented to help Churchill win the Second World War. In fact, they were preparing a trap for the Doctor – who inadvertently activated the New Dalek Paradigm, an officer class of Daleks which superseded the old creatures.

PRISONER ZERO

A prisoner of the Atraxi, Prisoner Zero escaped through a crack in time – into Amy's house.

The Weeping Angels were not statues – but actresses made up to look like stone, standing very still. And not blinking.

SMILERS

The security robots on *Starship UK*. The Smilers' heads revolved to change from a smiling face to an angry snarling one.

WEEPING ANGELS

The Eleventh Doctor encountered the Weeping Angels at the wreck of the spaceship *Byzantium*, and again in New York in the 1930s. A Weeping Angel took both Rory and Amy back into the past, where the Doctor could never see them again.

SATURNYNS

The last survivors of an aquatic race from the planet Saturnyne, only one female – Rosanna – and her male children survived the journey to Earth. Rosanna immediately set about finding brides for her sons.

SILURIANS

A group of Silurians was awakened by a drilling project at Cwmtaff. The Doctor tried to broker a peace, but without success, and the Silurians went back into hibernation.

The Silurians do not come from the 'Silurian' period of prehistory – that was a mistake made by a scientist who discovered them in their first story with the Third Doctor.

KRAFAYIS

Savage, invisible creatures. Only the painter Vincent Van Gogh could see the Krafayis that terrorised his neighbourhood.

DREAM MASTER

The Dream Master appeared to give the Doctor, Amy and Rory a choice of realities – if they chose the wrong one, they would die. But in fact neither reality was the true one.

THE ALLIANCE

An alliance of the Doctor's enemies and other aliens that thought the only way to save the universe was to imprison the Doctor in the Pandorica.

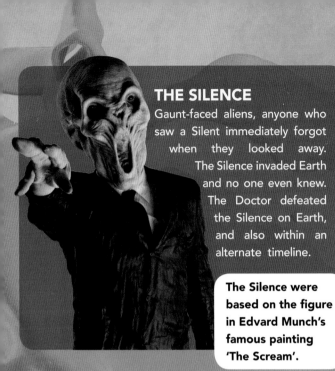

THE SILENCE

Gaunt-faced aliens, anyone who saw a Silent immediately forgot when they looked away. The Silence invaded Earth and no one even knew. The Doctor defeated the Silence on Earth, and also within an alternate timeline.

The Silence were based on the figure in Edvard Munch's famous painting 'The Scream'.

HOUSE

House was a sentience that wanted to capture a TARDIS to travel into the real universe. It took the soul of the Doctor's TARDIS – its very essence – and put it into the body of Idris. But, working together, the Doctor and Idris returned to the shell of the TARDIS and reclaimed it.

GANGERS

Copies of humans made from an organic substance called the Flesh. They even had the same memories as the originals – and rebelled, as they believed they ought to have lives of their own.

SIREN

A beautiful woman who appeared to Captain Avery and his crew – spiriting away any of them who were wounded. In fact, she was an automatic alien nurse taking them for medical treatment.

MADAME KOVARIAN

Madame Kovarian used the Flesh to create copies of both Amy and her child, Melody, and replace the originals. She worked with the Headless Monks and the Silence, among others, planning to destroy the Doctor who she saw not as a hero but a villain.

THE ORDER OF THE HEADLESS

Supposed to be unable to feel fear or to be deceived, the Headless Monks were part of Madame Kovarian's anti-Doctor alliance.

HANDBOTS

Medical robots at the Two Streams Kindness Facility on Apalapucia where they cared for patients infected with Chen-7. When Amy was trapped in the facility, she had to avoid the Handbots as their medication would kill her. She reprogrammed one Handbot and drew a face on him – she called it Rory.

PEG DOLLS

George, a Tenza child, trapped Amy and Rory in a doll's house where these creepy Peg Dolls played. Their touch turned Amy into a Peg Doll, too.

SOLOMON

A space trader and scavenger in the 24th century, Solomon found a Silurian Ark Ship. He murdered the Silurians, intending to sell the dinosaurs stored on the vessel.

WOODEN KING & QUEEN

The trees on a planet in the Androzani system were sentient. To escape being melted down for fuel with acid rain, they fashioned a wooden King and Queen to seek the help of the Arwell family.

THE SHAKRI

A race that eliminated species they deemed to be pests. They tried to destroy the human race, sending billions of small cubes to Earth to assess the population and then attack.

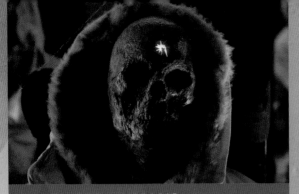

DALEKISED HUMANS

Converted into human–Daleks by nanocloud technology, these Dalek Agents appear like ordinary humans – until activated, when a Dalek eye-stalk grows from their forehead. They can also produce a gun from their hand.

DR WALTER SIMEON

When he was a child, the dark side of Walter Simeon's mind took over. Over the years, what had started as a reflection of himself took on a life of its own and became the Great Intelligence. Even after Simeon was killed, the Great Intelligence animated his body – and vowed revenge on the Doctor.

Richard E. Grant who plays Doctor Simeon has also played the Doctor – twice. Once, very briefly, in spoof adventure *The Curse of Fatal Death* (by Steven Moffat), and also in the animated webcast *Scream of the Shalka*.

THE GUNSLINGER

Military cyborgs – part humanoid and part machine – were created to serve as soldiers in a terrible war. One of the cyborgs – Kahler-Tek – was damaged and his original personality resurfaced. He tracked down and killed the scientists who had converted him into a cyborg – finding the last of them, Kahler-Jex, in the town of Mercy.

CYBERMEN

The Doctor and Craig found a Cybership that had crashed and been buried on Earth centuries ago. A surviving Cybermat drew power and sought 'spare parts' to create Cybermen. On Hedgewick's World, the Doctor and Clara witnessed the attempted birth of a new race of Cybermen. The Cybermen were all destroyed – or were they . . . ?

TIAANAMAAT MUMMY

For millions of years, the Long Song was sung to a mummy called Grandfather, on Tiaanamaat. But when it awoke, it wanted feeding with souls. To pacify the creature, it was offered the soul of the Queen of Years.

ICE WARRIORS

Grand Marshal Skaldak was trapped in Arctic ice, and discovered by the crew of a Soviet submarine. Thawed out, the Ice Warrior believed himself to be under threat and planned to trigger a world war in retaliation for the destruction of his people.

THE WITCH OF THE WELL

The ghost of Caliburn House on the Yorkshire Moors was actually a pioneering time traveller – Hila Tacorian. There was also another presence – an alien monster in search of its lover . . .

THE WHISPER MEN

Do you hear the Whisper Men? The Whisper Men are near. If you hear the Whisper Men, then turn away your ear. Do not hear the Whisper Men, whatever else you do. For once you've heard the Whisper Men they'll stop and look at you.

MRS GILLYFLOWER & MR SWEET

Sweetville in Yorkshire in 1892 was an idyllic place to work – except for the Crimson Horror. It was the domain of Mrs Gillyflower – apparent philanthropist. But actually she planned to use a prehistoric venom to enslave the world – provided by an alien lobster-like creature clamped around her neck called Mr Sweet.

THE TIME OF THE DOCTOR

All manner of different life-forms, including the Doctor, are drawn across space by a mysterious message. He eventually works out that the message is in fact a question: 'Doctor who?' It is a question obviously intended for the Doctor, and one that only he can answer – with his true name. The Time Lords have sent the message from the pocket universe where they are trapped, having survived the Last Great Time War. But if the Doctor answers them, they will return. And with the Daleks among others waiting for them, the Time War will begin again . . .

So instead of sending a reply, the Doctor makes it his mission to defend the place the message is coming from. He settles in the town of Christmas on the planet Trenzalore – the planet where he knows he will die. The Church of the Papal Mainframe ensures that no technology can get to the planet, but even so the Doctor has to defend it against Weeping Angels, Sontarans, and even a Cyberman made of wood.

Eventually, after Trenzalore has been besieged for centuries, the Daleks manage to invade. Knowing that he is in his final incarnation, the Doctor prepares to die. But then a huge crack opens in the sky, and the Time Lords bestow a new cycle of regenerations on the Doctor. He uses the regeneration energy to destroy the Dalek spaceship and defeat their attack. Then, back inside the TARDIS, he changes . . .

REGENERATION

In the Fourth Doctor story *The Deadly Assassin*, it was established that Time Lords only have twelve regenerations. With the revelation of the War Doctor's existence, and the 'meta-crisis' regeneration which created a duplicate of the Tenth Doctor, this means the Eleventh Doctor has actually run out of his maximum twelve regenerations. When this life comes to an end – as it does after centuries on Trenzalore – he should die.

But when Clara begs the Time Lords, trapped in their pocket universe, to help the Doctor, they do. They send him the energy for another complete cycle of regenerations. This not only enables him to regenerate into the Twelfth Doctor, but might also mean that he has many more regenerations yet to come . . .

THE TWELFTH
DOCTOR

The Twelfth Doctor was a much older-looking Time Lord than his predecessor. He was also rather less outgoing and personable. The influence of Clara Oswald in particular helped the Doctor to become a little more aware of other people's feelings.

Beneath his tetchy and unforgiving exterior this was the same Doctor as ever. He continued to fight against injustice and evil, and made it his mission to save whoever he could. In fact, his face was a constant reminder that he must save people. As he finally remembered in *The Girl Who Died*, the Twelfth Doctor had the same face as Caecilius – the Roman who the Doctor saved, together with his family, from the eruption of Mount Vesuvius in *The Fires of Pompeii*. This memory prompted the Doctor to save the life of a Viking girl named Ashildr.

Sadly, the Doctor had to let Clara go after the events of *Face the Raven*. He then encountered his wife, River Song, only to have to let her go as well after twenty-four years on Darillium. Throughout his last days he clung to the hope of reforming his arch-nemesis Missy, the Master's female incarnation, but in the end, he found the strength to let go of the most difficult thing of all: himself.

WHO IS THE TWELFTH DOCTOR?

Scottish actor Peter Capaldi has been a fan of *Doctor Who* right from childhood. He was an active member of the official *Doctor Who* fan club and sent letters to the show's production office during the Third Doctor's era.

A versatile and talented actor, he was perhaps best known for his role as Malcolm Tucker in the comedy series *The Thick of It* before landing the role of the Doctor. He has also appeared in the *Doctor Who* spin-off series *Torchwood*, as well as playing the character of Caecilius in the Tenth Doctor story *The Fires of Pompeii*. Capaldi is also an accomplished director, writing and directing the BAFTA- and Academy Award-winning short film *Franz Kafka's It's A Wonderful Life* for BBC Scotland in 1993.

DEEP BREATH

Still rather unstable from his regeneration, the Doctor brings the TARDIS to Victorian London, accompanied by Clara and a dinosaur. The Doctor and Clara stay with the Silurian Madame Vastra, her human wife, Jenny, and their Sontaran butler, Strax.

When the dinosaur is destroyed, the Doctor is determined to investigate. He and Clara find themselves in a restaurant run by clockwork robots. They are from the sister ship of the SS *Mme de Pompadour*, which the Tenth Doctor visited in *The Girl in the Fireplace*, and are continually repairing themselves with parts taken from human bodies.

The Doctor and Clara have to avoid being used for spare parts, as well as stopping the robots from killing anyone else . . .

INTO THE DALEK

The Doctor finds himself in the far future on board the spaceship *Aristotle*, which is being hunted by the Daleks. The humans on the *Aristotle* have captured a Dalek – a Dalek that has malfunctioned and seems to have developed a conscience.

The Doctor, Clara and several soldiers are miniaturised and injected into the Dalek's casing. Here they have to evade automated antibodies while the Doctor tries to discover what has happened to the Dalek. He finds a radiation leak that is slowly killing the Dalek creature. But when he fixes it, the Dalek reverts to its usual homicidal nature.

With a force of Daleks attacking and boarding the *Aristotle*, the Doctor and Clara need to save themselves as well as the human soldiers with them.

ROBOT OF SHERWOOD

When Clara asks the Doctor to take her to visit Robin Hood, the Doctor has to explain that the legendary outlaw is just a myth, a story – he never really existed. But when he takes Clara to Sherwood Forest anyway, a man claiming to be Robin Hood is the first person they meet. Although the Doctor remains unconvinced, it seems he was wrong about Robin . . .

Captured by the Sheriff of Nottingham, the Doctor, Clara and Robin discover that the Sheriff's knights are actually robots and that Nottingham Castle is a huge disguised spaceship. The robots are repairing the ship, but if it takes off it will destroy half of England. While Robin battles against the Sheriff – who is also partly robotic – the Doctor must find a way to stop the ship from exploding on take-off.

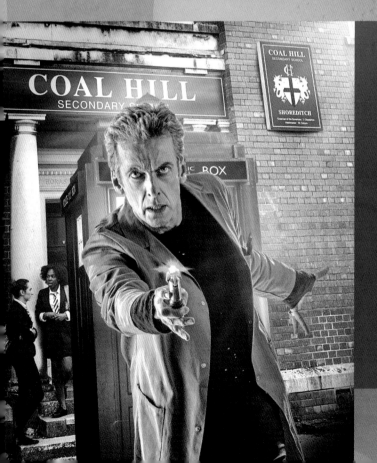

THE CARETAKER

Coal Hill School, where Clara teaches English, has a new caretaker – the Doctor. He has taken the job so he can lure a dangerous Skovox Blitzer to the school one evening when it's deserted, in order to deal with the alien robotic device.

But the Doctor has miscalculated. First of all, it's parents' evening, meaning that the school is full of teachers, children and parents. Secondly, Clara's boyfriend, Danny Pink, soon finds and turns off the chronodyne generators that the Doctor intends to use to send the Skovox Blitzer into the far future.

With the deadly Skovox Blitzer loose in the school, the Doctor has to come up with another plan to get rid of it, while Danny comes to terms with Clara's relationship with the Doctor.

MUMMY ON THE ORIENT EXPRESS

The Doctor and Clara arrive on board a version of the Orient Express from the future – a train that travels through space. But they soon discover that the train's passengers are in great danger. On board is the Foretold, a legendary creature that resembles an ancient Egyptian mummy. Anyone who sees the Foretold has just sixty-six seconds left to live.

The Doctor discovers that the Foretold is not on board by chance. Someone wants the people gathered on the train to study the creature. As the Doctor finally works out what the Foretold actually is, he has just sixty-six seconds to discover how to prevent himself from becoming its next victim.

DARK WATER/DEATH IN HEAVEN

When Clara's boyfriend, Danny Pink, is killed in a road accident, she tries to force the Doctor to save him. They find that Danny has been 'preserved' by the mysterious 3W organisation. At its hidden headquarters in St Paul's Cathedral, the Doctor and Clara meet Missy – who is actually a female incarnation of the Master.

Missy has been preserving the minds of the dead, planning to resurrect them as Cybermen. With Danny returned as a Cyberman, the Doctor has to find a way to stop more Cybermen being created by the Cyber Pollen that Missy is spreading across the planet. Whatever happens, will Clara be able to save Danny, or is he really gone forever?

THE MAGICIAN'S APPRENTICE/
THE WITCH'S FAMILIAR

The Doctor is missing. UNIT can't find him, and neither can Missy. Nor can Davros, who has sent his servant Colony Sarff to deliver a message to the Doctor. The Doctor, meanwhile, has been traumatised by the experience of meeting a young boy trapped in the middle of a minefield. He is about to save the boy when the child tells him his name – Davros. Can the Doctor bring himself to save the creator of his mortal enemies, the Daleks? Or will he leave a child to die alone on a battlefield?

When the Doctor is eventually found, he agrees to meet Davros. The Doctor, Clara and Missy are taken to Skaro, the planet of the Daleks. Davros claims he is dying and this is why he wanted to see the Doctor. But can Davros be trusted? Is he really nearing the end of his life, or is this all an elaborate trap?

With the Doctor having to decide whether or not to save the boy, Clara also has to decide if she can trust Missy after all . . .

UNDER THE LAKE/BEFORE THE FLOOD

The Doctor and Clara arrive in an underwater base called The Drum – and find that it is haunted. The ghosts appear to be silently mouthing the same phrase over and over again, and are also somehow connected to an alien spaceship recently discovered in the lake where the base is situated.

As the ghosts try to kill the surviving crew, the Doctor travels back to before the area was flooded in an attempt to find out what is going on. He discovers that the spaceship was a hearse carrying the body of the Fisher King. But the Fisher King is not dead, and is using the ghosts to send a message to his own people to come and rescue him – and to enslave the human race.

With Clara trapped in The Drum, and the Doctor's ghost joining the others, can he change his own future and defeat the Fisher King?

THE GIRL WHO DIED

Captured by Vikings, the Doctor and Clara are as surprised as anyone when the Norse god Odin appears in the sky above the Vikings' village. Odin takes the best warriors from the village to meet him in Valhalla. He also takes Clara and a young girl called Ashildr. But Odin is not what he seems. He is one of the Mire, a race of infamous conquerors, and Valhalla is a spaceship where he kills the warriors he captures.

When Ashildr voices her anger at what Odin has done, Odin returns her and Clara to the village, promising to come back with his own warriors and destroy the village and everyone in it.

The Doctor manages to form the surviving villagers into a motley fighting force. He feeds Ashildr's imagination into the Mire's vision systems in order to make a huge puppet monster seem real, scaring the Mire away. But the effort of creating the illusion kills Ashildr. Using Mire technology, the Doctor resurrects her. With the alien technology inside her body, constantly keeping her alive, Ashildr discovers that she can never die . . .

THE ZYGON INVASION/
THE ZYGON INVERSION

The Zygons have lived hidden among the population of Earth, disguised as humans, since the peace treaty brokered by the Tenth, Eleventh and War Doctors in *The Day of the Doctor*. But now a group of Zygons wants to end the peace and take over Earth for themselves.

The peace is dependent on the Osgood Box, overseen by the two versions of Osgood in existence since *The Day of the Doctor* – one human, one Zygon in human form. But one of them is dead, killed by Missy, and the other is being held prisoner by the Zygons. With Clara also a prisoner and her form taken by a Zygon out to assassinate the Doctor, can peace be restored? It's up to the Doctor and UNIT to prevent a catastrophic mass-unmasking of Zygons all around the world.

SLEEP NO MORE

The Doctor and Clara find themselves on the Le Verrier space station orbiting Neptune in the 38th century. The station seems deserted, until they meet a rescue team sent to find out why the station has gone silent. There is no sign of the crew.

A scientist called Rassmussen has been working on the station to improve the Morpheus technology that allows people to get the equivalent of a whole night's sleep in five minutes. But the sleep dust that builds up in the corner of the eye when someone is asleep has evolved into sentient creatures – Sandmen. Made up of human cells, they feed on people to create more of the dust from which they are made.

The Doctor and Clara have to save the rescue team and make sure that neither the Sandmen nor the enhanced Morpheus technology ever leaves the station.

FACE THE RAVEN

The Doctor and Clara's old friend Rigsy calls them for help. He has a tattoo on his neck, except he didn't put it there. The tattoo is a number – and it's counting down. In fact, the tattoo is a chronolock, and when it reaches zero, Rigsy will die.

The Doctor and Clara discover that Rigsy has found a hidden street in London. Here alien refugees gather, looked after and governed by Ashildr. She put the chronolock on Rigsy after he apparently killed a woman from the street. When his time is up, a Quantum Shade in the form of a raven will come for him and kill him.

But nothing is what it seems, and the street is actually a trap for the Doctor. A trap that will cost his best friend her life . . .

HEAVEN SENT/HELL BENT

The Doctor is transmatted to a strange castle and stalked by a mysterious veiled creature. He eventually finds a way out, through a wall harder than diamond which will take him billions of years to break. Every time the veiled creature kills him, the Doctor is reborn from the transmat, until eventually he breaks through the wall and finds himself on Gallifrey.

It was the Time Lords who trapped the Doctor. They want to know about the Hybrid, a creature prophesied to be an amalgam of two warrior races, and which would cause Gallifrey's destruction. On the Doctor's insistence, the Time Lords rescue Clara from the moment of her death. But Clara still isn't quite alive – rather, she is frozen in time, without a pulse, caught between her final heartbeats. The Doctor takes her to the end of time itself, where they meet Ashildr, but he is unable to make Clara's heart beat again.

To keep her safe, the Doctor plans to wipe Clara's memories of him. Instead, he ends up wiping his own memories of her – when he wakes up, he remembers Clara's name, but not what she looked like.

Unable to travel with the Doctor any more, Clara knows she must go back to Gallifrey to be returned to the point of her death. But she and Ashildr have a TARDIS, and Clara decides to travel back to Gallifrey the long way round . . .

THE HUSBANDS OF RIVER SONG

Still recovering from Clara's departure, the Doctor finds himself united with River Song on Christmas Eve. River doesn't recognise his new face and drags him, as a seemingly innocent bystander, into a high-speed adventure to steal the Halassi Androvar, the most valuable diamond in the world, from inside the head of the cyborg tyrant King Hydroflax. They flee with the diamond (and the king's irate head) to the starship *Harmony and Redemption*, which they then crash on the planet Darillium – in time to spend one final night together . . .

THE RETURN OF DOCTOR MYSTERIO

In New York City on Christmas Eve, the Doctor accidentally gives superpowers to a young boy named Grant. Years later, Grant works as a mild-mannered nanny watching over his childhood sweetheart's daughter. But by night, Grant fights crime as masked superhero, The Ghost.

The Doctor and Grant, aided by Grant's boss, Lucy, and the Doctor's assistant Nardole, must work to stop the evil Harmony Shoal Institute, and the brain-stealing aliens who run it, from destroying New York and invading the Earth.

THE PILOT

The Doctor has taken up residence as a university lecturer, while he and Nardole watch over a mysterious vault. When he learns that catering assistant Bill Potts attends all his lectures, the Doctor takes her under his wing. Bill's encounters with an enigmatic girl named Heather and a mysterious puddle soon draw her into the Doctor's world and set off a chase across time and space. The Doctor, Bill and Nardole eventually manage to discourage their pursuer, and Bill becomes the Doctor's newest companion.

SMILE

The Doctor sneaks away from Nardole and his duties guarding the vault to take Bill to a distant colony world – only to find that the colonists are all gone. They soon learn that microscopic robot builders, the Vardy, have been corrupted and begun killing anyone who isn't happy. With a ship full of frozen colonists to protect, the Doctor and Bill hurry to find a way to prevent further tragedy. The Doctor manages to reset the Vardy to clear the fault and leave them a sentient, independent species ready to cooperate alongside the humans who were formerly their masters.

THIN ICE

The Doctor's attempt to get himself and Bill back to the university before Nardole realises they're gone fails, and instead he takes them to the last London frost fair in 1814. Their enjoyment of the wondrous sights on the frozen River Thames is cut short by rumours of strange disappearances, and odd lights in the river. They soon discover a vast creature imprisoned under the ice, being used and exploited for the fuel it creates by the wicked Lord Sutcliffe, who plans to kill everyone at the frost fair to feed to the monster. The Doctor and Bill foil Sutcliffe's plan and free the creature, which cracks the ice as it escapes, and Sutcliffe falls to his death in the watery depths below. The Doctor then arranges for a group of urchins to inherit his house and estate.

KNOCK KNOCK

The Doctor helps Bill move into a new student house with a group of friends and soon comes to the conclusion that there is something very wrong. Bill's friends begin to disappear, and their charming landlord suddenly seems very sinister. Bill finds one of her friends being absorbed into the wood of the house, aided by the Landlord, while the Doctor finds evidence that Bill's friends are not the first students the house has eaten.

It turns out the house is filled with Dryads, a race of wood-dwelling creatures that are consuming Bill's friends to maintain the Landlord's daughter, Eliza, whom they saved from illness by converting her to wood. It turns out, though, that Eliza is the Landlord's mother, not his daughter, and has been kept alive far beyond her years. Eliza convinces the Dryads to let her and the Landlord die, restoring Bill's friends to life as the house collapses.

OXYGEN

The Doctor, Bill and Nardole arrive on Chasm Forge, a deep mining station in a future where oxygen is a regulated commodity. Able to breathe only when wearing the station's spacesuits, the TARDIS crew quickly discover that something is making the spacesuits kill their wearers. The Doctor, Bill and Nardole help the survivors to stop the killer spacesuits but, unknown to Bill, the adventure leaves the Doctor blind.

EXTREMIS

The Doctor is asked to look into a mysterious book that makes people kill themselves. Along with Bill and Nardole, he begins to investigate a text known as the Veritas, soon realising that they are all inside a simulation – and that he is not the real Doctor, but a simulated copy. The simulation is being run by an alien race called the Monks, as a test run for their invasion of Earth. The simulated Doctor sends a message to the real Doctor to warn him, while the vault's mysterious occupant is finally revealed to be Missy.

THE PYRAMID AT THE END OF THE WORLD

A 5,000-year-old pyramid appears where the three largest armies in the world are in dispute over territory. The Earth is soon presented with an offer by the Monks – submit to their will, or be destroyed. The Doctor, who is still unable to see, tries to prevent the approaching apocalypse before anyone can accept the deal. But when the Doctor's blindness leaves him about to die, Bill sacrifices the world's freedom to save the Doctor's sight . . . and his life.

THE LIE OF THE LAND

Now living in a world ruled by the Monks, Bill is found by Nardole and recruited to help rescue the Doctor. In search of a way to end the Monks' hypnotic hold on the world, the Doctor enters the vault and asks Missy for a way to stop them. Ignoring Missy's advice, the Doctor and Bill are able to end the Monks' rule by replacing their fake history broadcast (beamed around the world) with Bill's real memories and dreams of her mother.

EMPRESS OF MARS

When the words 'God Save the Queen' are found buried under the Martian ice-cap, the Doctor travels back to 1881 where he and Bill find a band of Victorian soldiers searching Mars for the untold mineral wealth of the Ice Warriors. They soon stumble upon the tomb of the Ice Empress Iraxxa and, when she and her warriors awaken, the Doctor must find a way to make peace between humans and Martians before they wipe each other out . . .

THE EATERS OF LIGHT

The Doctor and Bill argue over the fate of the lost Roman Ninth Legion so they travel back to Roman Britain to find out what really happened to them. They are separated, and Bill falls in with the Ninth Legion survivors, hiding underground from a monster that destroyed their comrades, while the Doctor and Nardole join with the Celts, who released that very monster – 'The Eater of Light' – into the world. The Doctor helps them lure the creature back through the portal to its own dimension, but hundreds more wait beyond the threshold to break through. The Doctor tries to sacrifice himself to keep them at bay, but Celts and Romans unite to stop him and give their own lives and futures to defend their shared planet.

WORLD ENOUGH AND TIME/THE DOCTOR FALLS

The Doctor decides to test Missy's desire to turn good by taking her on a trial run – to a Mondasian spaceship caught in the gravity well of a black hole. But Bill is shot and taken away by hooded figures in medical gowns to the far end of the ship, where time passes much faster. While the Doctor, Missy and Nardole make their way down to save her, Bill spends years waiting with the eccentric Mr Razor, while strange and sinister experiments are carried out on the other patients. The Doctor arrives too late, and finds Bill converted into a Cyberman, while Missy learns that Mr Razor is in fact her former self, the Master, in disguise.

When the Cybermen turn on them, Missy and the Master are forced to join forces with the Doctor, Nardole and the cyber-converted Bill to save the surviving humans on the ship. The Cybermen can be driven back, but the cost to the Doctor and his friends will be very great indeed . . .

THE TWELFTH DOCTOR'S COMPANIONS

CLARA OSWALD
Helped the Doctor
From: *The Bells of St John*
Until: *Hell Bent*
Played by: *Jenna Coleman*

Having become such a firm friend of the Eleventh Doctor, it took Clara a while to adjust to his new persona. But helped by advice from Madame Vastra as well as a phone call from the Eleventh Doctor himself, she soon came to appreciate that the Twelfth Doctor was indeed the same man she had always trusted. If anything, it was by becoming too much like the Doctor herself that Clara sealed her own fate.

THE PATERNOSTER GANG
Helped the Doctor
In: *Deep Breath*
Madame Vastra played by: *Neve McIntosh*
Jenny Flint played by: *Catrin Stewart*
Commander Strax played by: *Dan Starkey*

The Twelfth Doctor returned to Victorian London soon after his regeneration, while he was still unstable. But as ever he could rely on Madame Vastra, Jenny and Strax to help him – and to help Clara accept that this really was the Doctor. The Paternoster Gang also came to the rescue of the Doctor and Clara when they were captured by a group of homicidal clockwork robots.

UNIT
Helped the Doctor In:
Death in Heaven
The Magician's Apprentice
The Zygon Invasion
The Zygon Inversion
Kate Stewart played by: *Jemma Redgrave*
Petronella Osgood played by: *Ingrid Oliver*

UNIT has been as ready to call on the Twelfth Doctor for help as they have any other Doctor. UNIT's Chief Scientific Officer, Kate Stewart – daughter of Brigadier Lethbridge-Stewart – has asked the Doctor for help against the Cybermen, tried to find him when planes froze in the sky, and enlisted his help again when it looked as if the peace treaty with the Zygons was about to fall apart.

DANNY PINK
Helped the Doctor In:
The Caretaker
In the Forest of the Night
Dark Water
Death in Heaven
Last Christmas
Played by: *Samuel Anderson*

Maths teacher at Coal Hill School where Clara Oswald taught English, Danny Pink was an ex-soldier who became Clara's boyfriend. Although wary of her relationship with the Doctor, Danny eventually came to accept it. Clara was devastated when Danny was killed in a road accident. But his mind was stored by Missy and he came back, briefly, as a Cyberman. The depth of Clara's feelings for Danny became clear when, having been attacked by a Dream Crab, her dream of an ideal life was Christmas spent with Danny.

COURTNEY WOODS
Helped the Doctor
In: *The Caretaker*
           Kill the Moon
Played by: *Ellis George*

One of the more disruptive of Clara Oswald's pupils at Coal Hill School, Courtney Woods met the Doctor when he was working at the school as caretaker. Despite her being sick when the Doctor took her in the TARDIS to see the stars, he did take Courtney on another trip – to the moon. But that wasn't straightforward either, as Courtney encountered giant bacteria that looked like spiders, and discovered the moon was actually an egg about to hatch.

ROBIN HOOD
Helped the Doctor
In: *Robot of Sherwood*
Played by: *Tom Riley*

Although the Doctor believed that Robin Hood was just a legend, he and Clara met Robin in Sherwood Forest. Just as the stories said, Robin led a band of outlaws against the Sheriff of Nottingham. But the Sheriff was aided by robot knights from a spaceship that had crash-landed and was now disguised as Nottingham Castle. With Robin's help, the Doctor and Clara were able to stop the spaceship from destroying the whole area when it tried to take off.

PERKINS
Helped the Doctor
In: *Mummy on the Orient Express*
Played by: *Frank Skinner*

Chief engineer on the future Orient Express that travelled through space, Perkins helped the Doctor unravel the mystery of the Foretold. As well as supplying a list of all the passengers, a plan of the train and a list of all the train's stops in the last six months, it was Perkins who gave the Doctor a vital clue as to why people died exactly sixty-six seconds after first seeing the Foretold. When the Doctor offered him the chance to travel in the TARDIS, Perkins politely declined.

ASHILDR
Helped the Doctor
In: *The Girl Who Died*
The Woman Who Lived
Face the Raven
Hell Bent
Played by: Maisie Williams

When the Doctor used Mire technology to bring the Viking girl Ashildr back to life, he made her in effect immortal. Over the years she founded a leper colony, became a queen and faked her own death, survived the Black Death and fought at Agincourt (disguised as a man). She met the Doctor again when she was a 17th-century highwayman known as The Knightmare. In the present day, she organised a refugee camp for aliens hidden in London and met the Doctor and Clara again, with disastrous consequences . . .

RIGSY
Helped the Doctor
In: *Flatline*
Face the Raven
Played by: Joivan Wade

A graffiti artist from Bristol, Rigsy met Clara when they encountered the two-dimensional Boneless. Rigsy's own aunt was one of the victims of the Boneless, and he helped Clara and the Doctor defeat them, creating a picture of a door that the Boneless thought was real. The energy they directed at it recharged the miniaturised TARDIS, allowing the Doctor to get out. Rigsy also called for the Doctor and Clara's help when he found he had a mysterious number tattoo. It was actually a chronolock, counting down to his death. Clara saved Rigsy's life, but at a terrible cost . . .

NARDOLE
Helped the Doctor
From: *The Husbands of River Song*
Until: *Twice Upon a Time*
Played by: Matt Lucas

An assistant to Professor River Song when the Doctor first met him, Nardole lost his head to the cyborg body of King Hydroflax in *The Husbands of River Song*. The Doctor rebuilt him and kept him around as a friend and assistant. River Song gave him express permission to 'kick the Doctor's arse if needs be'. Nardole ended up staying with the surviving humans on the Mondasian colony ship.

BILL POTTS
Helped the Doctor
From: *The Pilot*
Until: *Twice Upon a Time*
Played by: Pearl Mackie

Originally a canteen worker at the university, Bill's keen intelligence and enthusiasm for learning led the Doctor to sponsor her enrolment as a student. He became her personal tutor (on the condition that Bill never got less than a first) and she soon joined him on numerous adventures across time and space. She never let him down, even when she was converted to a Cyberman on the Mondasian colony ship. They got a last goodbye, of sorts, in the Doctor's final adventure as his twelfth incarnation.

RIVER SONG
Helped the Doctor
In: *The Husbands of River Song*
Played by: Alex Kingston

River thought she knew all of the Doctor's faces, so she didn't recognise the Twelfth Doctor when she met him. Once she realised it was him, they were able to spend one last night together on the planet Darillium – happily for both the Doctor and River Song, a night on Darillium turned out to last twenty-four years.

GRANT

Helped the Doctor
In: *The Return of Doctor Mysterio*
Played by: *Justin Chatwin*

The Doctor appeared on Grant's windowsill on Christmas Eve when Grant was a child. He gave him an intuitive gemstone to hold, which Grant mistook for medicine and swallowed. The gemstone gave Grant superpowers and, years later, he fought crime as The Ghost, a masked superhero, while also working as a nanny for Lucy.

LUCY FLETCHER

Helped the Doctor
In: *The Return of Doctor Mysterio*
Played by: *Charity Wakefield*

A single mother and reporter for the *Daily Chronicle*, Lucy was at school with Grant and later hired him as a nanny to look after her daughter, Jennifer. She investigated the Harmony Shoal Institute, where she met the Doctor and Nardole, as well as encountering Grant in his superhero identity as The Ghost.

HEATHER

Helped the Doctor
In: *The Pilot*
The Doctor Falls
Played by: *Stephanie Hyam*

Heather was a fellow student of Bill's, and the two grew close until Heather encountered a space-travelling alien oil that absorbed her and made her its pilot. Heather had promised not to leave Bill and so pursued her across space, until convinced to let her go. She later returned to save Bill's life, and the two kissed before travelling off to see the universe together.

ERICA
Helped the Doctor
In: The Pyramid at the End of the World
Played by: Rachel Denning

Erica was a scientist who accidentally helped create a deadly bacterium that could have ended life on Earth. She helped the Doctor destroy the bacterium before it could escape.

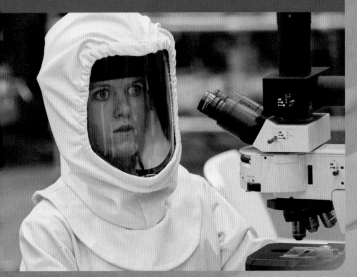

COLONEL GODSACRE AND FRIDAY
Helped the Doctor
In: Empress of Mars
Godsacre played by: Anthony Calf
Friday played by: Richard Ashton

Colonel Godsacre commanded the Victorian mission to Mars with the help of his Ice Warrior guide, Friday. Together, they convinced Iraxxa to make peace with the humans and Godsacre swore himself to her service.

KAR
Helped the Doctor
In: The Eaters of Light
Played by: Rebecca Benson

The last Keeper of the Gate, Kar went through the portal with the survivors of the Ninth Legion to keep back the Eaters of Light. Ravens across the world still remember Kar by speaking her name, so her sacrifice won't be forgotten.

CAPTAIN ARCHIBALD HAMISH LETHBRIDGE-STEWART
Helped the Doctor
In: Twice Upon a Time
Played by: Mark Gatiss

The Captain met the First and Twelfth Doctors wandering the South Pole, having been taken out of time at the moment of his death. The Twelfth Doctor altered history to save the Captain's life, then learned that the Captain was the grandfather of his old friend the Brigadier.

MISSY AND THE MASTER

MISSY

Fought the Doctor

In:
Dark Water
Death in Heaven

Helped the Doctor

In:
The Magician's Apprentice
The Witch's Familiar
Extremis
The Lie of the Land
Empress of Mars
The Eaters of Light
World Enough and Time
The Doctor Falls

Played by: Michelle Gomez

A female incarnation of the Master, Missy had a plan to turn dead people into an army of Cybermen. She then wanted the Doctor to be her friend again and, still seeing her as his friend, it was to Missy that the Doctor sent his confession dial when he believed he was about to die. But while supposedly helping the Doctor and Clara on the planet Skaro, Missy tried to trick the Doctor into killing Clara while she was trapped inside a Dalek casing. Missy was then supposed to spend a thousand years in the vault, but the Doctor released her, believing she could turn good – which, unknown to him, she eventually did.

THE MASTER

Played by: *John Simm*

Thrown out of Gallifrey by the Time Lords, the Master ended up stranded on the Mondasian colony ship. He engineered the genesis of the Cybermen, but when they turned on him he was forced to ally with the Doctor and his future self, Missy, to survive. In the end, he and Missy abandoned the Doctor, but when Missy decided to go back, the Master killed her, while she, in turn, killed him.

CLOCKWORK ROBOTS

The clockwork-powered repair droids from the SS *Marie Antoinette* used parts of people to repair themselves. The Doctor and Clara narrowly avoided being cannibalised for spare parts when they visited a restaurant in Victorian London run by the robots.

DALEKS

As well as being miniaturised in order to travel inside a Dalek in the far future, the Doctor also returned to the Dalek City on their planet, Skaro. The Daleks were working with Davros to trick the Doctor into making them even more powerful.

THE SHERIFF OF NOTTINGHAM

Unexpectedly discovering that Robin Hood actually existed, the Doctor also met Robin's nemesis, the Sheriff of Nottingham. But while Robin was, despite the Doctor's theories, a real person, the Sheriff had been turned partly into a robot. His knights were also robots – whose ship had crashed on Earth and which they had disguised as Nottingham Castle.

SKOVOX BLITZER

One of the most dangerous weapons ever created, the Skovox Blitzer was a robot built for war. When a Skovox Blitzer arrived on present-day Earth, the Doctor lured it to Coal Hill School in the hope of sending it into the far future where it could do no harm.

THE FORETOLD

A legendary killer, the Foretold was actually a soldier augmented with technology so that he did not die. His camouflage systems meant that no one could see the soldier, who was decayed and bandaged like an ancient Egyptian mummy – except for his next victim, who had just sixty-six seconds to live once the Foretold appeared to them.

THE BONELESS

Creatures from a flat, two-dimensional universe, the Boneless, as the Doctor named them, crossed through to our universe. They could make things and people two-dimensional, and tried to take on three dimensions. At first the Doctor thought that they were killing people by accident, but in fact they knew exactly what they were doing.

CYBERMEN

The Cybermen created by Missy were made out of the bodies and stored minds of the dead. She used Cyber Pollen to resurrect corpses and build a huge Cyber army, but a Cyber version of Danny Pink led the Cybermen to self-destruction.

Later, the Doctor met Cybermen who had evolved on a colony ship from the planet Mondas, with the aid of the Master. When the Doctor changed their understanding of the definition of human to include Time Lords, they turned against the Master and tried to convert him and Missy into Cybermen, along with their human victims.

DREAM CRABS

Dream Crabs feed on the brains of their victims, clamping over their faces. To make their prey easy to digest and kill, they induce a dreamlike state in the people they attack. So Clara, for example, thought she was enjoying an idyllic Christmas with Danny Pink – whereas in fact Danny was dead and she was slowly being killed by one of the Dream Crabs.

DAVROS

As he was dying – or so he claimed – Davros sent his servant Colony Sarff to find the Doctor. When the Doctor journeyed to Skaro, the home planet of the Daleks, Davros claimed to want to settle their differences at last . . .

THE FISHER KING

The Fisher King led armies that conquered the planet Tivoli and enslaved its people, ruling over them for ten years. After his apparent death, the Fisher King was taken to Earth to be buried. But in fact he was not dead, and started killing people to create ghosts that would project a message to his armies, telling them where to find him so that they could come and enslave the people of Earth.

ODIN AND THE MIRE

One of the most dangerous and formidable races of warriors in the galaxy, the Mire attacked a Viking village where the Twelfth Doctor and Clara had been taken. Masquerading as the god Odin, the Mire leader took away the village's warriors and killed them. But the Doctor was able to defeat Odin and his warriors by making a large wooden puppet appear to them as a terrifying monster.

ZYGONS

The Zygons have the ability to make themselves look human. Ever since a peace treaty was brokered by the Tenth, Eleventh and War Doctors, Zygons have lived on Earth disguised as humans and fitting into society. But when a group of Zygons decided that they wanted to end the peace and take over Earth, the Doctor, Clara and UNIT had to respond.

SANDMEN

When people sleep, a crust of mucus builds in the corner of their eyes, made largely of skin cells and also blood cells – sleep dust. Rassmussen's enhancements to the Morpheus sleep technology, which allowed people to get the equivalent of a full night's sleep in just five minutes, hastened the evolution of this sleep dust. The dust became sentient, and could form into hideous creatures – Sandmen – which were hungry and killed people to get more human cells from which to create more of themselves.

SHOAL OF THE WINTER HARMONY

A race of alien brains who stole the bodies of others, the Shoal of the Winter Harmony were loyal servants of the cyborg conqueror Hydroflax. They tried to acquire the Halassi Androvar diamond to honour Hydroflax. Another group of the Shoal posed as an international corporation and tried to invade Earth by destroying New York and luring world leaders into their headquarters to have their bodies stolen.

THE VARDY/EMOJIBOTS

The Vardy were microrobots created to terraform planets and build new human colonies. They used robots that could read human emotions as their interface. When these Emojibots misinterpreted grief as the enemy of happiness, the Vardy tried to eliminate this emotion by destroying any colonists that appeared to be unhappy.

HYDROFLAX

King Hydroflax, the Butcher of the Bone Meadows, was a cannibal cyborg with a detachable head. When his head was stolen by the Doctor and River Song, his body pursued it, stealing Nardole's and Ramone's heads on the way, before ultimately destroying his original head and trying to steal the Doctor's.

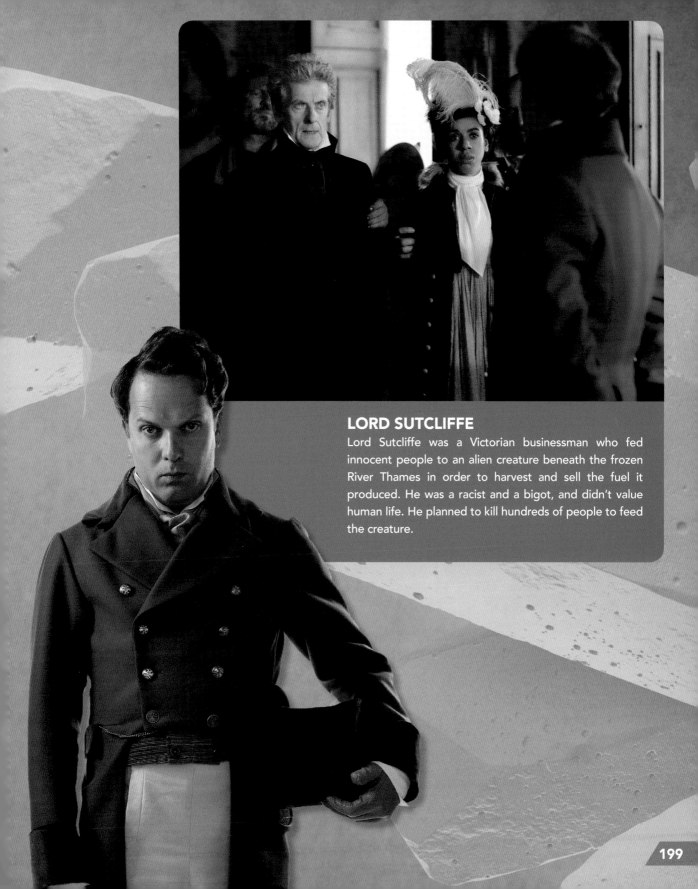

LORD SUTCLIFFE

Lord Sutcliffe was a Victorian businessman who fed innocent people to an alien creature beneath the frozen River Thames in order to harvest and sell the fuel it produced. He was a racist and a bigot, and didn't value human life. He planned to kill hundreds of people to feed the creature.

THE MONKS

The Monks were unusual invaders, requiring consent in order to conquer a world. They ran a simulation of the Earth to plan their invasion, which led the simulated Doctor to warn his real-world counterpart about the imminent attack. When the Monks conquered the Earth, they created a false history to make it appear as if they had always been there.

CAPTAIN NEVILLE CATCHLOVE

Captain Catchlove was Colonel Godsacre's second in command, and had actually been blackmailing his superior for years. He took command of Godsacre's soldiers, tried to fight the Ice Warriors and then took Iraxxa hostage in order to make his escape.

THE EATERS OF LIGHT

Monsters from a dimension of darkness, the Eaters of Light try to break into other dimensions to devour the light they contain. They came through a portal in a cairn in Scotland, but were driven back by the Keeper of the Gate and the Roman Ninth Legion.

EMPRESS IRAXXA

Queen of the Ice Warriors, Iraxxa, slept for 3,000 years before being awoken by the Victorian Mars expedition led by Colonel Godsacre. She planned to wipe out the human invaders until Godsacre saved her life. When she realised what Godsacre had done, she decided to spare the expedition, and welcomed their service on the planet.

THE END OF THE TWELFTH DOCTOR

TWICE UPON A TIME

Fighting not to regenerate, the Doctor is brought by the TARDIS back to the time and place of his first-ever regeneration. There he meets his first self, also fighting not to regenerate, and the two of them are soon joined by a displaced British Army captain from World War One. Time itself freezes and the two Doctors have to work together to protect the Captain from Testimony, the mysterious glass woman pursuing him.

Testimony offers the Doctor a chance to reunite with Bill, who quickly joins the Doctors in their escape with the Captain. Seeking more information on Testimony, the Twelfth Doctor learns from Rusty the 'good' Dalek that Testimony isn't evil, it's a research project preserving people's memories in the instant before death. Bill is really an avatar of Testimony, another glass figure that has taken Bill's form and memories.

Eventually, the Doctors acknowledge that they must return the Captain to the time and place of his death. Once they arrive, the Twelfth Doctor reveals he's nudged the timings slightly to save the Captain's life, and has placed him in the moment just before the Christmas truce of 1914. It turns out that the Captain is, in fact, the future grandfather of Brigadier Lethbridge-Stewart, helper and ally of the Doctor. Bidding farewell to his former self, and to his former companions through Testimony (including Clara), the Doctor returns to his TARDIS and finally regenerates.

REGENERATION

The Twelfth Doctor lived longer than any other. When the end came, he stated that he was tired of living, and fought against regenerating. His adventure with his first self and his reunion (of sorts) with Bill, Nardole and Clara convinced him that he could keep going.

The Twelfth Doctor, unlike his predecessors, took the time to address a set of rules to his next self. He advised them never to be cruel or cowardly (and never to eat pears), and reminded them that hate is always foolish and love is always wise. He told them never to reveal their name, as no one but children would understand it anyway. Finally, he told them to 'laugh hard, run fast and be kind', before finally letting go and regenerating into the Thirteenth Doctor. Her first words, as she sees her new face for the first time, are: 'Oh, brilliant!'

THE THIRTEENTH
DOCTOR

The Thirteenth Doctor is the first of the Time Lord's incarnations to be female – something which she reacted to immediately with 'Oh, brilliant!' Her friends are important to her, and she quickly became attached to Yasmin, Ryan and Graham.

The Thirteenth Doctor is full of wonder and excitement, and more considerate of the feelings of others than previous Doctors – but she has the same steel, determination and cunning. Sometimes, beneath her bright and breezy exterior, there are glimpses of the ancient and powerful being she is, and hints of hitherto-unsuspected darkness in her past; but it's important to her, as the Twelfth Doctor exhorted her before regenerating, to be kind.

WHO IS THE THIRTEENTH DOCTOR?

Jodie Whittaker was born in Skelmanthorpe, West Yorkshire in 1982 and attended the Guildhall School of Music and Drama, where she won the Gold Medal for Acting. After a string of impressive roles in films like *Venus* and *Attack the Block*, and television series like *Broadchurch* and *Trust Me*, she was announced as the first woman to play the Doctor in July 2017.

Showrunner Chris Chibnall, who wrote *Broadchurch*, encouraged Whittaker to audition for the Doctor after she had suggested she play a villain on the show.

THE WOMAN WHO FELL TO EARTH

A mysterious alien pod appears in the woods outside Sheffield, where it is discovered by Ryan Sinclair and Yasmin Khan. Meanwhile, a bizarre tentacled biomechanical entity appears on a commuter train and is driven off by a woman who falls from the sky through the roof of the carriage. She's the Doctor, and she's here to help.

Brutal Stenza warrior Tzim-Sha emerges from the pod. He is hunting for a human trophy to win the leadership of his people. Tzim-Sha had sent ahead the tentacled creatures, called Gathering Coils, to seek out his random target: crane operator Karl Wright. The Doctor and her new friends, Ryan and Yaz and Grace and Graham O'Brien, track Tzim-Sha across the city to try to stop the Stenza warrior. In a deadly showdown at a construction site, the Doctor confronts Tzim-Sha. She saves Karl's life but, tragically, Grace falls to her death from a crane while neutralising the Gathering Coils.

With the danger passed, the Doctor turns her attention to recovering her TARDIS, but her home-made transmat rig malfunctions. The Doctor, Ryan, Graham and Yaz are teleported into the depths of interstellar space . . .

THE GHOST MONUMENT

In the nick of time, the Doctor and her friends are rescued by Angstrom and Epzo, starship pilots and the last two competitors in the Rally of the Twelve Galaxies. The long-distance race has crossed ninety-four different planets so far, and they're on the final leg: a trip across the surface of the hellish planet Desolation to locate the enigmatic Ghost Monument. The Doctor recognises the monument – it's the TARDIS! She sets off to find it with her friends, Angstrom and Epzo.

Desolation holds many dangers, from flesh-eating water to remorseless SniperBots and the insidious Remnants, legacies of Stenza weapons research. But despite the planet's cruelty, the Doctor leads the group to the finish line unscathed. There, Angstrom and Epzo, who have bonded during the journey, demand to share the prize. The rally's organiser, Ilin, reluctantly agrees, and the Doctor is reunited with her beautiful Ghost Monument.

ROSA

The TARDIS transports the Doctor, Ryan, Yaz and Graham to Montgomery, Alabama, in 1955 – not modern-day Sheffield – where artron energy is flooding the city. When the Doctor bumps into seamstress Rosa Parks, she concludes that someone is attempting to meddle with history. Rosa will spark the Montgomery bus boycott, a protest against racial segregation that will become a key moment in the civil rights movement. But a racist murderer from the far future, Krasko, has acquired time-travel technology and he plans to prevent Rosa's protest, thereby altering history for the worse. It's up to the Doctor and her friends to make sure that things unfold as they should.

Thanks to a behaviour-modifying implant given to him in prison, Krasko is unable to directly harm anyone. He and the Doctor play a cat-and-mouse game of manipulation and trickery – one the Doctor eventually wins. Rosa Parks's moment of heroism goes unchanged, and Ryan zaps Krasko back to prehistory with his own time-travel weapon.

ARACHNIDS IN THE UK

The Doctor manages to bring the TARDIS back to Sheffield. It's only been half an hour, but many adventures, since they left. The Doctor is sad to say goodbye to her new friends, but she cheers up when Yaz invites her to tea.

One of Yaz's neighbours, Anna, is missing, and her work colleagues are concerned. The Doctor lets herself into Anna's flat to investigate. She discovers Anna's body on her bed, cocooned in spider silk. The spider itself, a common domestic species, has somehow grown to the size of a dog. Meanwhile, Graham has returned home to a giant spider, too.

The Doctor investigates and discovers that Sheffield is a hotbed of unusual spider activity. She traces the epicentre to a luxury hotel being built by American billionaire Jack Robertson, whose illegal dumping of toxic waste has caused the city's spiders to mutate. With the help of her friends – and the music of Stormzy – the Doctor ends the arachnid threat once and for all.

THE TSURANGA CONUNDRUM

An accident with a sonic mine leaves the TARDIS crew in need of medical attention, and they find themselves on board a Tsurangan medical transport. But the ship has an unwelcome stowaway: the dreaded Pting, one of the most dangerous life-forms in the galaxy. The invulnerable Pting is tiny but voracious, and it's eating its way through critical parts of the ship. Even if the Pting could be stopped, the ship's fail-safe system has set a time bomb for self-destruction in order to stop the creature reaching the Tsuranga hub.

The Doctor and her friends work out that the Pting feeds on energy of all kinds, and they lure it to an airlock filled with power-packed explosives. With the Pting and the bomb jettisoned into space, the crew manage to steer the ship home.

DEMONS OF THE PUNJAB

When Yaz asks to learn more about her grandmother Umbreen, the Doctor takes her to the Punjab in 1947. It is just before the partition of India – the country is about to be split in two. The new India–Pakistan border will divide families and neighbours who have known each other for generations. And Umbreen is getting married to Prem – a Hindu man who is not Yaz's grandfather.

Meanwhile, the Doctor investigates sightings of shadowy aliens connected to the death of a local holy man who was to marry Umbreen and Prem. The Doctor identifies the aliens as Thijarians, a notorious race of assassins, and she confronts them with the crime. The Doctor learns the Thijarians are no longer murderers – they now act as witnesses to lonely deaths throughout history. The holy man was in fact murdered by Prem's militant younger brother, Manish. As the chaos and violence of partition engulfs the Punjab, the Doctor oversees Umbreen and Prem's wedding. Soon after, Prem bravely stands up to Manish, but he is killed. Umbreen leaves Pakistan to seek a new life in Sheffield.

KERBLAM!

A strange android appears in the TARDIS with a package for the Doctor. It's a Kerblam Man – a teleporting postman from Kerblam, the gigantic intergalactic retailer. Inside the package is a fez the Doctor had ordered, but also a chilling note: HELP ME . . .

On the moon of Kandoka, Kerblam's headquarters, the Doctor and her friends learn of a sinister series of disappearances among the downtrodden human workforce. They discover that the artificial intelligence that runs Kerblam was behind the call for help – it knows something is deeply wrong.

The TARDIS crew investigates and discovers that Charlie Duffy, a janitor, is the mastermind. He is a terrorist infiltrator who wants to highlight the plight of human workers in an age of robotics. He has booby-trapped the bubble wrap in Kerblam's parcels to destroy anyone who pops it. But the Doctor is able to foil his plot, and she restores Kerblam's AI to full functionality.

THE WITCHFINDERS

The TARDIS arrives near Pendle Hill, Lancashire, in 1612, where the Doctor and her friends stumble across an elderly woman being 'ducked' in the river. She has been accused of witchcraft by local magistrate Becka Savage. Although the Doctor is too late to save the old woman, she fools Savage into thinking that Graham is the witchfinder-general.

King James, who is travelling around the country on a personal crusade against witches, arrives in Pendle Hill and takes charge. At the same time, recent victims of the witchfinders are coming back to life as eerie, malevolent mud creatures. The Doctor discovers that Becka Savage is infected with the alien influence that is reviving the dead. Then, the Doctor is accused of being a witch herself . . .

The Doctor escapes her own ducking and confronts Becka, who reveals that she has been possessed by aliens called the Morax. Becka cut down an ancient oak on Pendle Hill and accidentally released the Morax, who had been imprisoned inside. With the help of King James and a branch from the oak tree, the Doctor forces the Morax back into their hidden prison.

IT TAKES YOU AWAY

The Doctor and her friends discover an isolated cabin in a Swedish forest, where teenager Hanne lives with her father, Erik. But Erik is missing, and terrifying noises in the woods around the house suggest something monstrous is lurking in the dark.

Soon, the TARDIS crew discover that the noises are sound effects. Erik has set up speakers outside to deter Hanne from leaving the house, and he has disappeared through a portal in the mirror in the attic. The Doctor, Yaz and Graham venture through while Ryan looks after Hanne. The portal leads to the Antizone – a dark and dangerous cave-like half-world between two universes. Despite Flesh Moths and the tricks of Ribbons, an untrustworthy goblin-like inhabitant of the Antizone, the Doctor makes it through the portal. In the other universe, she discovers Erik and his late wife living in a mirror-image of his home in our universe.

Erik's wife is in fact the Solitract – a sentient universe that is terribly lonely. It wants company, and it even transforms into Graham's late wife, Grace. The Doctor persuades Graham and Erik to leave because the two universes are incompatible and would destroy each other. Erik is reunited with his daughter, and for the first time Ryan calls Graham his grandad.

THE BATTLE OF RANSKOOR AV KOLOS

A cluster of distress signals draws the Doctor to the planet Ranskoor Av Kolos, where she discovers a vast field of wreckage from crashed spacecraft. A psychic field blankets the planet, causing disorientation and amnesia. The Doctor is able to protect herself and her friends, and also Paltraki, an alien pilot they meet wandering the surface.

Paltraki is contacted by a familiar enemy: Tzim-Sha the Stenza warrior. He demands Paltraki return a strange artefact to him – a sphere floating in a cube. Following his previous encounter with the Doctor, Tzim-Sha teleported to Ranskoor Av Kolos by accident. Luckily for him, he met the native Ux: a race of only two beings, both with godlike psychic powers. The wily Stenza warrior fooled the Ux into worshipping him and for more than 3,000 years he has used their power and Stenza technology to extend his life. With the Ux, Tzim-Sha has been shrinking planets and bottling them in stasis cubes – a deadly revenge that he plans to use on Earth next.

The Doctor convinces the Ux to abandon Tzim-Sha, and she averts the destruction of Earth. Meanwhile, Ryan and Graham work together to lock the Stenza warrior in a stasis chamber forever.

RESOLUTION

Archaeologists working beneath Sheffield Town Hall discover something strange buried far underground: unidentifiable pieces of organic matter. When exposed to ultraviolet light, the find comes back to life and more pieces teleport in from their resting-places at the four corners of the Earth. The reassembled and reanimated life-form is a Dalek scout, defeated hundreds of years ago and dismembered so it could not return to plague humanity.

The Dalek mutant has no cyborg shell, but it is able to latch on to one of the archaeologists, Lin, and control her like a puppet. It forces her to build a makeshift Dalek shell and blazes a path of destruction to GCHQ, the secret government telecommunications hub, where it plans to signal the Dalek fleet.

The Doctor and her friends race against time to stop the Dalek scout. They are only successful with the help of Ryan's estranged father, Aaron. The Doctor brings the Dalek into the TARDIS, then ejects it into the heart of a supernova, destroying it once and for all.

THE THIRTEENTH DOCTOR'S COMPANIONS

YASMIN KHAN

Helped the Doctor
From: *The Woman Who Fell to Earth*
Played by: *Mandip Gill*

A trainee police constable from Sheffield, Yaz is drawn in to the Doctor's world when she is sent to investigate reports of a mysterious object in the woods – an alien artefact that her old school friend Ryan Sinclair has stumbled across. As a police officer, she is observant, level-headed and always keen to help – though travelling with the Doctor offers her far more interesting possibilities than police work.

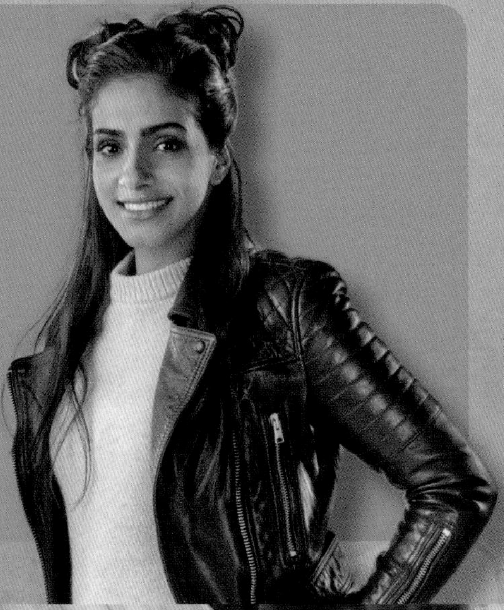

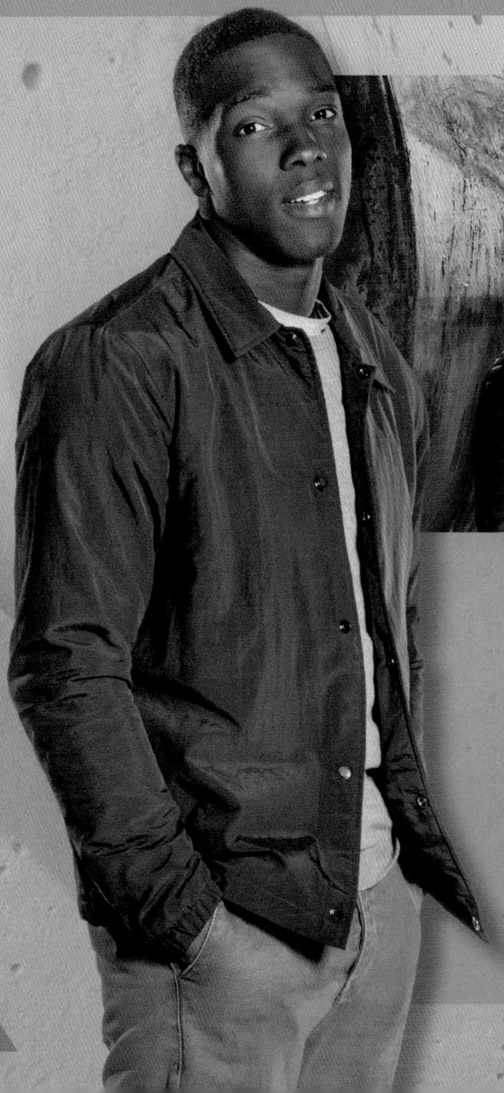

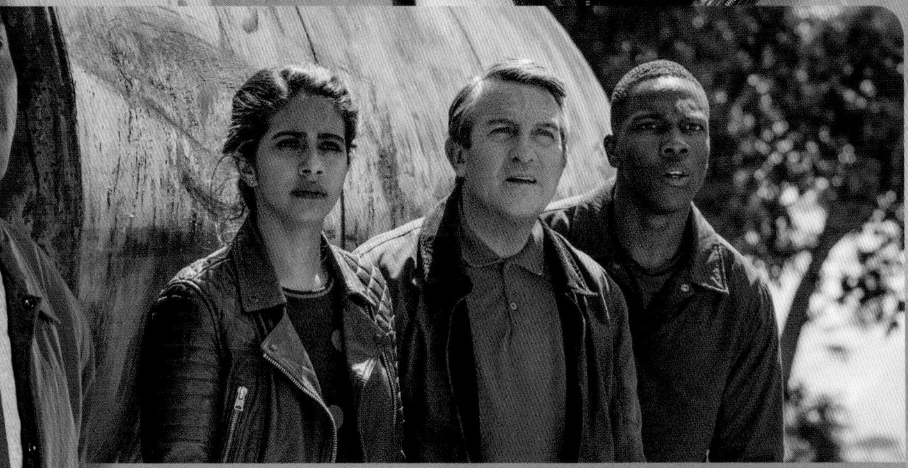

RYAN SINCLAIR

Helped the Doctor
From: *The Woman Who Fell to Earth*
Played by: *Tosin Cole*

Ryan meets the Doctor when she falls through the roof of the train he's travelling on and saves him from the Stenza's Gathering Coils. Following the tragic death of his grandmother Grace, who raised him, Ryan forms an uneasy relationship with Graham, his new grandad. Ryan is dyspraxic and struggles with his coordination. He's also a keen student of engineering, and he is fascinated by the Doctor's technology.

GRAHAM O'BRIEN

Helped the Doctor

From: *The Woman Who Fell to Earth*
Played by: *Bradley Walsh*

A retired bus driver from London, Graham O'Brien became ill with cancer, and during his treatment he fell in love with his nurse Grace. When Graham's cancer went into remission, he married Grace and moved to her hometown, Sheffield. Graham travels with the Doctor partly because of the grief he feels following his wife's death. He's also able to forge a bond with Ryan, who is all he has left of his beloved Grace.

GRACE O'BRIEN

Helped the Doctor

In: *The Woman Who Fell to Earth*
Played by: *Sharon D Clarke*

Grace's courage, heart and intelligence would have made her a perfect addition to the TARDIS crew, but she sacrificed herself to save Yaz and Ryan from the Stenza's Gathering Coils.

TZIM-SHA

The Stenza are a powerful warrior race, conquerors of the Nine Systems and wielders of advanced technology. The leadership of the Stenza is determined by a ritual: the warrior must travel 5,000 galaxies away and hunt down a human trophy. Tzim-Sha arrives on Earth to stalk his unwitting prey . . . only to encounter the Doctor.

GATHERING COIL

This is a bizarre biomechanical device used by the Stenza to gather data and hunt prey. Gathering Coils can join together in a swarm, becoming even more dangerous. They are vulnerable to electric shocks.

THE REMNANTS

Sinister beings that resemble strips of cloth, the Remnants were the creation of the Stenza science colony on the planet Desolation. They hunt at night, entangling and smothering their victims. They can also read minds, a power they use to mock and terrify their prey.

SNIPERBOTS

These deadly androids, armed with laser rifles, stalk the ruins on the cruel planet Desolation. Although relentless and accurate, SniperBots are not highly intelligent and they can be tricked.

ILIN

The master of the Rally of the Twelve Galaxies, Ilin was himself a former winner of the race, having battled his way across the stars to seize its fabulous prize. He is a cold and ruthless individual who was perfectly happy to see the Doctor and her friends perish on Desolation.

KRASKO

Krasko was one of the galaxy's most dangerous criminals, a mass killer and fanatical racist with 2,000 murders to his name. He was imprisoned in the Stormcage Containment Facility, where he was implanted with a neural restrictor that prevented him from harming any living thing. Using a vortex manipulator, he travelled back in time to try to meddle with history . . .

MUTANT SPIDER

Scientists experimented with common spiders, then disposed of the bodies of their genetically modified test subjects. The spiders ended up in Jack Robertson's illegal toxic-waste dump. Revived by the chemical cocktail, they began to grow uncontrollably. The largest spider, 'Mother', was the size of a truck.

JACK ROBERTSON

A ruthless billionaire whose luxury hotel was built on top of an illegal dumping-site for toxic waste. Robertson's greed and callousness led to Sheffield becoming infested with mutant spiders. He was only saved by the Doctor's intervention – not that he showed much gratitude.

PTING

The Pting is one of the most feared and dangerous life-forms in the universe – despite its diminutive size and harmless appearance. Invulnerable to all known forms of damage, the ravenous Pting seeks out and devours whatever energy it can find, relentlessly chewing its way through entire starships.

THIJARIANS

Once, the Thijarians were known as a race of assassins. They used their telepathic powers and mastery of teleportation to become the galaxy's most efficient killers. But their home planet was destroyed, and now the last two remaining Thijarians travel to bear witness and provide comfort to those who die lonely deaths.

KERBLAM MEN

The Kerblam Men are android delivery bots and the mascots of the company Kerblam. With their jaunty uniforms and fixed plastic smiles, they teleport directly to their destinations to deliver packages. They have even managed to appear aboard the TARDIS in flight!

CHARLIE DUFFY

Kerblam is an almost entirely automated company. There's little need for humans, and people like Charlie Duffy are forced to scrabble for the few menial jobs available. Disgruntled, Duffy became a human-rights terrorist who reprogrammed Kerblam's systems to deliver deadly explosives to its customers . . .

BECKA SAVAGE

Becka Savage was the landowner of Bilehurst Crag, a village in Lancashire, in the early 17th century. After cutting down a tree on Pendle Hill that was, unbeknownst to her, the lock keeping the Morax imprisoned, she was infected by the Morax queen. Out of terror, she began a local crusade against 'witchcraft'.

THE MORAX

Billions of years ago, the malevolent race known as the Morax was imprisoned for war crimes in a hidden jail beneath Pendle Hill in Yorkshire. They are mud-like, shapeless entities with the power to infect and possess both the living and the dead.

RIBBONS

A mysterious denizen of the Antizone between our universe and the Solitract, Ribbons of the Seven Stomachs was a sinister and untrustworthy guide to the Doctor and her friends, who later tried to betray them.

FLESH MOTHS

Deadly carnivorous insects native to the Antizone that can strip a victim to the bone, Flesh Moths are attracted to light and motion, and when they discover prey they shriek to summon the swarm.

THE UX

A unique species that numbers only two individuals, the Ux command unlimited psychic powers to reshape reality. The Ux worship a being known as the Creator, and when Tzim-Sha crashed on Ranskoor Av Kolos, they mistook him for their god. They wielded their power to extend his life and helped him wreak his revenge on the universe.

RECONNAISSANCE DALEK

Even by Dalek standards the Reconnaissance Dalek is a fearsome creature. Bred to scout and infiltrate planets for conquest, Recon Daleks are stealthy and almost impossible to kill. Even cut into pieces, the Dalek mutant is capable of teleporting back together and regenerating.

The Recon Dalek that menaced Sheffield had lost its travel vehicle, but it was able to control a human host, Lin, by plugging directly into her nervous system. Using Lin, it built itself a crude but serviceable shell. It was cunning enough to trick its way on to the TARDIS, before the Doctor was able to destroy it.

THE FUTURE

With her friends Yasmin, Ryan and Graham aboard the TARDIS, the Doctor sets out . . .

The Doctor has all of time and space stretching out before her, and exciting new escapades will be waiting wherever she travels. There are worlds out there where the sky is burning, where the sea's asleep and the rivers dream, people made of smoke and cities made of song. Somewhere there's danger, somewhere there's injustice and somewhere else the tea is getting cold.

Never cruel, never cowardly, always saving others and running towards the next adventure, she will forever be . . .
      the Doctor.